BEST FRIEND'S BROTHER'S SURPRISE BABY

KIRA COLE

1

AURORA

I wiggle my toes in the clear, salt water pool, looking over at my best friend's perfectly manicured feet and then nudging her with my shoulder.

"Thanks for inviting me out," I tell her, and Francesca Andretti grins, nudging me back and brandishing her champagne glass full of half bubbly and half orange juice. I'm halfway through my second mimosa myself, and feeling a little tipsy.

But I don't get out much. I'm usually home taking care of my ailing father. He's not been the same ever since a heart attack when he was only forty, and I've taken over most of the household stuff. Luckily, as a low-level wiseguy, he made enough money before he got too sick to take care of us. I'm grateful to him for so many things.

Francesca is like the sister I've never had, my best friend ever since we were twelve and crazy about every boy in junior high. I look over at Francesca. Her long, bleached blonde hair is almost white with the sunlight streaming through the glass pool enclosure, and her eyes are the prettiest sea-green color. She's always been prettier and skinnier than me, but I'm not exactly jealous.

For a while, it made me a little sad, that most of the guys I wanted looked at her first, but it's not Francesca's fault that she was born beautiful. And soon I grew out of it. I don't need the attention of anyone who is shallow enough to only care about a pretty face and a nice body. I have many qualities, and if the right guy comes along, he'll see beyond the rounder body and the average face. He'll see *me.* Too bad the right guy must be living under a rock, because all the guys that cross my paths have been wrong, wrong, wrong.

Marco Barone comes over toward us and I slide a little to the right side, trying not to grimace. Marco's attractive enough, but there's just something about him that makes me feel...uncomfortable. Francesca and I grew up around wiseguys, around bruisers, were raised by them, but Marco can be *ruthless.* The stories I've heard... A shiver runs down my back.

I worry about my best friend sometimes, that her beauty may get her into real trouble someday, because unlike me, she revels on the attention her beauty gets her. She has no problem with guys only wanting her for how she looks, she just wants to live life and have the best time she can.

Marco scoops her up into his arms and Francesca giggles and drops her mimosa glass. I catch it in a truly inspired bout of reflexes, but neither of the lovebirds notice. Finally, Marco finishes kissing her and puts her down.

"I gotta go now, *belissima,*" he says in a low tone, and Francesca pouts.

"All right, if you must."

Marco scoffs. "If you want me to keep you in diamonds, I have to."

Francesca grins and flips her damp blonde hair. "You bet I want you to keep me in diamonds."

"The staff will lock up when you leave," he says flippantly and kisses her fiercely once more before walking back into the house.

Francesca shrugs and comes back to the pool, slipping into the water and dunking her head before beginning to tread water, splashing at me.

I laugh and slide into the water with her and we swim and play for a bit before she gives me the most mischievous smile.

"Oh no," I say, knowing what that means. "What are you doing, Francesca?"

"So listen," she begins, and I already want to roll my eyes. I know this is going nowhere good, with that look on her face. "The Espositos are having a party tomorrow night."

"You mean Bruno is having a party tomorrow night," I say dryly, and she bites her lip, grinning.

"Exactly."

"Marco's only out of town for a couple of days," I warn. "Don't you think this is a bad idea?"

"What Marco doesn't know won't hurt him," she says easily.

I hum. She and Marco aren't exactly *exclusive*, especially given that Marco has been seen with several other girls over the six months they've been dating, but I would bet my life savings that he expects Francesca to be exclusive with him. That's just the way wiseguys are.

"I don't know," I hedge, and Francesca pouts.

"Come on, Aurora. I know you're going to come with me to keep me out of trouble, so let's not have this back and forth," she says, and I hate that she's right.

Francesca is my best friend and like a sister to me, and I

wouldn't ever want her to be in trouble or risk losing her. I don't have many people in my life, so I want to keep the people I have close.

I sigh and heave myself out of the pool. I look at my empty glass of mimosa. "I guess I'll get an Uber," I say, and Francesca scoffs, coming up the pool ladder.

"No way. I'll call Nico," she says, and my breath catches in my throat.

Nico Andretti.

Same sea-green eyes as my best friend, but this time with the longest, darkest lashes, the strongest Roman nose, a square jaw, and the fullest mouth. Nico Andretti is absolutely gorgeous and I've had a crush on him since before I was fourteen.

Not that Francesca will ever get that information out of me. And not that it matters anyway since I'm invisible to him.

"Sure," I say easily, trying to push down the lump that's in my throat.

Since I'm not driving or having to schedule an Uber, I suck down another mimosa quickly, needing the liquid courage to see and talk to Nico.

"So, Bruno bought me a tennis bracelet," Francesca chatters away and I'm barely listening. "But I can't wear it in front of Marco. So, I thought I'll get Marco to buy me one, too, then he won't know the difference!" She titters and I frown in her direction.

"Francesca," I start, but then I realize I'm still in a bikini when Nico's car pulls up, and I rush to put on a pair of shorts and my tank top. I manage to get dressed before he walks in, thank God, coming in the back of the pool house and waving, jerking his head as if he's irritated.

I hurry over to his car while Francesca takes her time.

"Thank you for the ride, Nico," I say, and he grunts in response, getting in the driver's side and revving the engine to make Francesca hurry up.

She takes her sweet time anyway, just to be a brat, and I chuckle as I slide into the backseat.

"You should have called shotgun," Nico says, and I can't help the blush that spreads across my cheeks.

"I don't mind the backseat," I say, and Francesca gets into the passenger side.

"You're driving us to the Espositos tomorrow night, right?"

Nico groans. "I've got to be there anyway. Dante is invited. So, I guess I'll drop you off."

Francesca grins. "Perfect."

Nico raises an eyebrow at her as he pulls out of the driveway. "You know, Marco isn't going to like you going to Bruno's."

"Marco is out of town," she says breezily.

"You're going to get yourself in trouble one of these days, you know that?" Nico warns, but Francesca just scoffs.

"I'm just having fun," she argues, and I look out the window so that I stop staring at Nico's profile.

I had the biggest dreams of growing up and marrying him when I was a teenager, and it all seems so ridiculous now.

As if he would ever want me.

"I'm going to drop you off first," Nico says to Francesca. "I'm on my way to Dante's and Aurora's place is on the way."

I swallow hard. I'm going to be alone in the car with Nico, which makes the blush on my cheeks deepen and redden.

I know I should be over my little crush by now, but I can't help it.

He's just so...Nico.

He's unlike anyone I've ever met before. I wish that I had someone like him in my life, like a boyfriend or a husband. I've always wanted a family, and I don't feel like I'll ever have one.

"You're going to the Esposito party?" he asks me, looking at me in the rearview mirror.

I nod slowly, keeping eye contact. God, his eyes are so pretty, his stare intense.

"Keep her out of trouble," he says, giving me a little smile, and my heart skips several beats.

"Trouble is my middle name," Francesca chirps, and she waves her fingers at me as Nico pulls up at their place.

She lives in a pretty house. It's just Francesca and their ailing mother living there now. Nico has his own apartment and comes to visit often. Their father had done pretty well for himself before he was killed, so the house was all theirs. He hadn't ever wanted to be anything but low level, but still he provided for his family. Gave them a roof.

My dad was the same. And I wouldn't have it any other way. At least I don't have to worry about watching my back and having someone come after my family.

I'm glad that my father was just a low-level thug and not a made man.

"Get in the front," Nico says as Francesca makes her way to the front door. It's almost demanding and it sends a shiver down my spine. I do as he says and climb over to get in the front seat, my arm brushing against his.

"I'm glad you're going to be at the party," he says, and I blink, looking over at him as I buckle my seatbelt and he pulls out into the road.

"You are?"

"You always watch out for her. Gives me less work to do," he says, and I swallow, feeling slightly disappointed.

What else would he say? That he wants me to go because he's secretly in love with me? I feel stupid.

Nico's quiet the rest of the way home but when I get out of the car after we pull up, he calls my name softly. I freeze and turn.

"You're a good friend," he says simply, and I walk inside with the memory of his intense gaze, the way he'd said my name so softly.

I really have it bad.

2

NICO

I can think of about five things I'd rather be doing (three of them women) that isn't standing around at Bruno Esposito's stupid party. It isn't even really a wiseguy party, just something that Bruno has thrown together for his birthday. I end up not picking up Aurora because Francesca insists on coming early and Aurora has to finish getting ready, so I just take my sister to the mansion. She runs off the second we arrive.

The mansion is huge, probably bigger even than Dante's. The Espositos are an old family, and Bruno is the next in line. I guess that's part of the reason that Francesca likes him so much. She's attracted to power, that's for sure.

I'm the guy that works for the men in power, and I like it that way. There's too much responsibility in being a made man. Too many people trying to take what you have. I'm glad I'm under the radar and don't have to worry about looking over my shoulder at every turn.

Esposito parties have a reputation about being a little wild, and while, sure, that's exciting, I prefer to do my partying in private. It's not like I can't let loose, but part of being under the radar means not drawing attention to your-self. I don't like being in the public eye because that's not what I want for my life. I want to just live how I want and not have to worry about looking over my shoulder all the time.

These made men and their heirs, they don't care what people think of them. They do whatever they want, when they want, and that's what draws women like my sister to them.

She wants that kind of freedom, the one we've never had since we come from the lower-level thugs and drivers. What my sister fails to understand is that isn't freedom at all – not when people are after what you have. I just want to protect what's mine.

We couldn't be more different, but I love Francesca with all my heart and promised my father I'd take care of her.

I sigh, looking around for said little sister, but she's nowhere to be found. She's probably off somewhere with Bruno. I'm grateful that Marco's out of town, because he's a bit of a hothead.

I'm probably being generous. He's more like a loose cannon.

Francesca is playing with fire, and she's bound to get burned, so I'm glad that her much more level-headed best friend is here to help me out.

Just like me and Francesca, Aurora and my little sister are very different, even though they're both still young and immature.

Opposites attract, I guess.

As I'm scanning the room yet again looking for Francesca, my eyes land on a woman coming down the stairs. Her legs are thick and tanned, leading up to a little white club dress that hugs her generous curves. Her hips are wide and I can't help licking my lips as I look up at her. Women could be my weakness, if I allowed them to mean anything to me.

I don't.

They are a liability. An anchor that forces you to stay in one place. A distraction, though that can be both a welcoming quality and a flaw, depending on the occasion. But most of all, they are a weapon that can be used against you. If you take a chance on love, you are giving someone else the power to hurt you, directly or indirectly, and I can't afford that. Especially as Dante's security man. I'd be putting both of us at risk.

But just because I'll never fall in love doesn't mean that I stay away from them. I love women and they love me, so we have fun together but the stakes are always clear. I like to enjoy a nice pair of legs, ample cleavage, or a wide pair of hips for a night, but that's as far as it goes. They know not to expect more.

I've always been attracted to curves, and this woman has them in spades. Her cleavage spills out of the low-cut top.

As I'm staring, she stumbles, her hair falling down across her face.

I take the steps two at a time and steady her with a hand on one hip and she looks up at me with a smile.

Shit.

Aurora.

I blink at her, shocked that I've just been checking out my little sister's best friend, and I let my hand linger on her hip a little too long.

"Jesus, Aurora," I mumble. "That dress—"

She blushes and looks down at herself. "I know, it's too tight. Francesca talked me into it. I should have changed."

I shake my head fiercely, taking her chin in my hand and tilting it upward.

"No, you look amazing," I tell her, and her deep brown eyes search my face as if to see if I'm lying.

"You really mean that?" she asks softly.

"I do," I say in a low murmur, looking her up and down again, unable to help myself.

Aurora blushes and braces herself against the wall.

"I guess I should find Francesca," she says, and I let go of her hip reluctantly, watching her walk the rest of the way down the stairs, staring at her legs and ass.

When did Aurora Costa get so *hot*?

She's just a kid, I remind myself. *Your little sister's best friend, you dog.*

In my own defense, I *am* kind of a dog. I take advantage of my good looks whenever opportunity arises. That's one of the reasons I can't blame Francesca for playing Marco and Bruno, I guess.

Maybe Francesca and I are more alike than I realize.

A hand claps me on the shoulder and I turn, dragging my gaze off of Aurora's ample ass, and see Dante standing there, with a very pregnant Mia, smiling at me.

"You picked out your newest conquest?" he teases, and I shake my head.

"Nah, nothing like that. That's Francesca's best friend. She'll look out for her tonight."

"Good to know. I need you to focus on work tonight," Dante says in a low tone. Mia doesn't like hearing about business.

I nod. Dante wants me to corner Bruno Esposito and ask him how he feels about the Gallos. Between Dante and Luca Lorenzo, Mia's father, they'd taken out the Gallos recently.

I need to know if anyone is thinking of avenging the

Gallos, but I really think Dante's just being paranoid about Bruno.

The Espositos were never friends with the Gallos and hated them as much as we did, as far as I know. But Bruno is the new heir and his father is ailing, not even coming down for the party, and I guess we need to know if the new blood in the family feels differently.

Dante and Mia make it down the stairs to mingle and I head up the stairs, looking around for Bruno. There are people milling around upstairs and I don't find him, but I do find Angelo Bianchi.

Angelo does some muscle work for Dante here and there. We've been friends since high school, when we played basketball together, but I haven't seen him a few months.

"Nico," he says warmly, pulling me into a brief hug. "It's been a while."

"Not long enough," I say dryly, but then I break out into a smile.

Angelo laughs. "You bring a date?" he asks, and I shake my head.

"Do I ever? Need to keep my options open," I say, and Angelo shakes his head, smiling.

"You never change," he chuckles.

"Never will," I say matter-of-factly. "Have you seen Bruno anywhere?"

Angelo shrugs. "He could be anywhere, you know Bruno. Probably partying somewhere in a bathroom."

Bruno isn't a stranger to hard drugs, so it's not uncommon to find him doing lines in a bathroom. I let out a long breath.

At least he'll be talkative.

"Thanks," I mutter, and walk toward the balcony on the second floor. I look down at the people in the yard, seeing if

I can catch sight of Bruno, but no such luck. I don't see Francesca, either, so I assume they're together.

I wrinkle my nose. I don't want to walk in on that, so maybe I should just take a break. I pull out a pack of cigarettes from my jacket. It's a habit I'm trying to break, so I only smoke once every blue moon, now, when things are really bad.

I put the cigarette in my mouth but don't light it. I like to just feel it there. I satisfies the craving somehow.

I keep thinking about that body on Aurora. How come I haven't ever noticed?

She's too young for you, I tell myself. *Stop it.*

But the image of her tanned, thick thighs is tattooed beneath my eyelids when I close my eyes briefly.

I've got to get it together.

AURORA

I've never been particularly popular, but there must be something to this dress, because men keep coming up to me, introducing themselves.

Alessandro Barone, Marco's younger brother, walks up to me, looking me up and down.

"What's your name, pretty girl?" he asks in a low tone, and I snort out a laugh.

"You've known me since high school, Alessandro. I was the year ahead of you? We were in choir together?"

He just looks at me blankly.

"Aurora Costa," I say, sighing, and his eyes widen.

"No fucking way," he says in a mumble, and for the first time I notice his eyes are a bit glassy. I don't smell booze, though, so I suspect drugs.

"You've been hanging out with Bruno too much," I accuse, and Alessandro shrugs, smirking.

"Maybe. I can't believe I didn't recognize you," he says, stepping closer. I back away, not wanting to get cornered by him.

"I guess that's a compliment?" I say dryly.

"Of course it is. Look at you," he says, licking his lips. "I never noticed you before, but that *dress...*"

"Well, you can go back to not noticing me again," I say flatly. "I'm looking for Francesca," I say finally, wanting to get to her before she starts doing lines, as well. I hate it when she does hard drugs, she turns into a person that I don't really like. I know that Nico worries about her, too.

"I saw her with Bruno in his office earlier," he says, and I nod, making my way up the stairs, teetering a little in Francesca's tall heels. I can't believe I let her talk me into this outfit and these shoes, but here I am.

I walk past Dante and his wife, Mia, and I smile at her swollen belly. I've always wanted kids of my own, but I'm not sure that it's in the cards for me since guys tend not to notice me. Usually.

I push the thought out of my mind, not wanting to think about that while I'm trying to have fun at a party. I guess I have been having fun, especially when Nico gave me a compliment. I can still feel his hand on my chin, how he tilted my face up to his like he was going to kiss me. I have to keep myself from shuddering in pleasure just thinking about it.

Did he really think I looked beautiful tonight? Francesca's giggle sounds from inside a room with an open door as I walk down the hallway. I smile, rolling my eyes.

I knock on the doorjamb and Francesca is in Bruno's lap and they are both sniffling, so I know they've been partaking in Bruno's stash.

"Aurora!" she cries, standing up and coming toward me, hugging me tightly. She also smells like that fruity wine she loves, so I guess she's been partying hard. "Let me pour you a glass of wine."

I take the glass but only take a small sip, looking over at

Bruno who is just gazing adoringly at Francesca. If I were to pick which of the men Francesca is seeing for her, I'd probably pick Bruno.

Marco is a violent man, and I've heard some horror stories, while Bruno is younger, a sweet guy for the most part, even though he may have a bit of a drug problem. That's not unusual in his line of work, though, and he's certainly got the money and support for rehab if he ever needs it.

Marco may be more straight-edge, only partaking in a couple of drinks socially and never overdoing it, but his personality is a lot more cut-throat, and I think Francesca deserves someone who looks at her the way that Bruno does. Not like he owns her, like Marco does, but like he just loves every move she makes.

I wish I had that.

I wish Nico would look at me like that.

I flush just thinking about it and take another gulp of my wine.

"We were about to put on some different music," Francesca says, wrinkling her nose. "The stuff they're playing downstairs is so...*old*."

I chuckle. Classical music plays quietly downstairs, and I guess she's right, it's centuries old. She puts on a record, some hip-hop song, and bounces around to the music, shaking her hair all around.

Bruno looks at her like she's the only woman in the room, and I can't help but smile. I hope in the end, she chooses Bruno.

Francesca finishes her wine and then pulls me into dancing with her. I laugh and sway along with her, moving my hips and taking hold of hers to dance with her. Francesca is always fun, and that's one of the reasons that we've always been so close.

Another reason is that she's always been there for me, good and bad times.

She's never made me feel like lesser, even though sometimes I feel like I'm in the shadow of her great looks and big personality, and I'm grateful to her for being my friend.

Bruno stands up and starts to dance behind Francesca and she leans back against him. He kisses her throat and I cough to make my presence known.

"Get a room," I mutter, and Francesca belly-laughs and pushes away from him.

"She's right," she says. "I'm here with Aurora, you know? She's really my date." She links her arm through mine, leaning her head against mine. She's taller and thinner than me, but we fit together well.

I smile at Bruno and he smiles back but only has eyes for Francesca.

"Isn't this dress gorgeous on her, Bruno?" she asks, and Bruno nods but he's still looking at Francesca.

"Everyone's complimented me on it," I say. "Even Nico."

Francesca's eyes widen. "Even my brooding brother says it's a nice dress? You really are *wearing* it, then, Aurora!"

I smile at her and she leads me over to the desk, where there's a mirror and white lines spread out on the table.

I feel myself go pale.

"You know that I don't like this kind of stuff, Francesca," I mutter, and she pouts.

"I know, Aurora. I'm just having a little fun," she says and does a line. I frown but at least she's not pushing me to try it.

I know that my mother has issues with addiction, or at least she did before she disappeared on us, so I never want to put myself in that kind of situation.

I look out through the window and see a familiar-looking car pulling up. I frown even deeper and grab Francesca's arm.

She sniffles and stands, looking out the window.

"Tell me that's not..." I trail off and look at Francesca, who goes instantly pale.

"Shit," she curses under her breath, and grabs onto my arm, dragging me out into the hallway and into a closet with towels and linens folded up on the shelves. She puts a finger to my lips.

"Be quiet," she whispers.

I groan inwardly but keep my mouth shut. It's Marco's car I saw pulling up through the gates, and I should have known that he would get wind of this. Francesca is in trouble now, and I need to try and keep her out of it, as much as I can.

We stand in the closet for what seems like forever, and finally I put my hand on the doorknob.

Francesca grabs my arm and pulls me back toward her. "Don't go out there," she hisses.

"I just want to talk to them," I say calmly. "Maybe I can keep Marco from beating him up too bad."

Francesca nods, her perfectly manicured brows drawn together. "You're right," she breathes. "You're calm and you can talk to them. I can't go out there, though."

I nod. "I don't want you to," I reassure her and hug her tightly before opening the door.

I shut it behind me quickly and hurry toward Bruno's office. He's sitting in his chair, facing Marco, whose shoulders are stiff.

"So, you're fucking my girl," Marco says slowly, and a grin spreads across Bruno's face as I watch from the doorway.

I swallow hard, about to say something, when Marco

pulls out his gun and shoots Bruno directly in the face. There is hardly any sound, with the party still going. That's when I notice the gun has a silencer.

Bruno jerks once, and his head is tilting up, as if he is staring at the ceiling, but the thin red trail coming down his forehead tells me the bullet was true to its mark.

I make a squeaking sound in the back of my throat and that's when Marco turns around, locking eyes with me.

A scream builds in the back of my throat and I look around desperately but it's just the two of us. Everyone else is either downstairs or on the balcony.

Marco advances toward me and I do the only thing that I can think of – I run, sprinting past Francesca who's come out of the closet.

"Aurora," she yelps as I push past her, but I ignore her. She didn't see anything, so she isn't in danger right now. I am.

I've got to get the hell out of here before Marco turns that gun on me.

4

———

NICO

I'm still outside smoking, not paying much attention to the rest of the party, when a blood-curdling scream cuts through the night. It takes me only a second to realize that it's Francesca, and my heart begins to pound as I run down the hallway. I have to push people out of my way, most of the party had started to move upstairs and everyone was in the way. Now that Francesca had screamed, people were all going that way and I all but elbowed everyone out of my way as I approached Bruno's office.

Francesca is standing in the doorway, shivering all over and I put my hands on her shoulders, turn her away from Bruno's dead body.

"Shit," I curse.

Francesca clutches on to me, making me look at her. "It was Marco," she whispers. "You have to get to Aurora. She saw everything."

Fuck.

Apparently, there's a witness to this murder, and it's my little sister's best friend. I'm going to have a long night ahead of me, clearly. I take Francesca's shoulders in my hands and look at her fiercely.

"Find Dante," I say. "Stay with him and Mia until him or me tell you otherwise. Do *not* go back to the house."

She nods quickly, tears streaming down her face. "You'll find Aurora? Keep her safe?"

"I'll find her," I promise.

I make my way outside easily because everyone is going upstairs to see what the commotion is. I don't see Marco, thank god, but I see that there's a piece of white dress in the woods, hanging on to a branch. *Aurora.*

I grab the piece off the branch and head into the woods, ignoring the cuts and scrapes from the branches and thorns. I catch sight of her in the middle of the forest, doubled over and panting, and I come right up behind her and grab her with one arm around her waist and the other clamped over my mouth.

She goes stiff all over in my arms and I whisper in her ear, "It's me, Nico." She slowly relaxes into my arms. I add, "I'm going to get you somewhere safe."

My head is spinning. I know that Marco is a loose cannon, but at the same time, I didn't think he'd kill Bruno in such a public manner. It seems like Aurora is the only real witness to the murder, so Marco will be after her.

"He just shot him," Aurora mutters. "His eyes, Nico....they were crazed..." she says, trembling all over, and I scoop her up in my arms, carrying her toward my car. Everyone's inside, trying to figure out what happened, and I suspect that Marco's still in the woods, looking for Aurora.

I put her in the front seat, buckling her seatbelt.

She's covered in scrapes from the woods and there are leaves and sticks in her hair. She's all but hyperventilating.

Shit.

What a turn this night has taken, from me appreciating Aurora's figure to trying to save her life.

"He saw me," she mumbles. "He saw me see him, and he's going to kill me, Nico."

"No, he won't," I say firmly. "No one's going to hurt you while I'm around," I promise.

Aurora looks at me and I cup her chin in my hand again.

"Look at me," I tell her as her eyes dart around nervously. She looks into my eyes. "Everything's going to be okay," I say slowly. "You're safe."

"I'm safe," she repeats in a low voice, but she's still trembling when I drop her chin and pull out of the driveway, tires screeching as I get on the main road. It's another ten minutes before she speaks again. "Where are we going?"

"Somewhere safe," I say simply. There are half a dozen safehouses between here and the city, and I plan on using them. Dante has given me the keys, after all, and in the meantime, he'll keep Francesca safe.

"Where's Francesca?" Aurora asks suddenly. "Is she okay? We have to go back," she says, clutching at my forearm.

"She's okay," I tell her quickly. "She's with Dante."

Aurora lets out a sigh of relief. "Oh, thank god."

Then she promptly bursts into tears.

I make it another six miles away from Bruno's before I pull over, unable to take the sounds of her sobs anymore, and draw her into my arms.

"It's going to be okay," I tell her softly, stroking her dark hair. "I'm going to keep you safe."

She doesn't answer, just shaking and pressing her face into my chest, getting my silk shirt wet, but I don't give a fuck.

She's just a kid and she's been through so much tonight. The least I can do is comfort her.

When her sobs turn into sniffles, I let her go and put the car back into gear, pulling back out onto the road.

"It's about an hour drive. Try and get some rest," I tell her, and Aurora remains quiet but she doesn't sleep, just looking listlessly out the window.

I take a deep breath, unable to believe what has happened in such quick succession. I'm stuck with my little sister's best friend, trying to keep her alive, all because my sister couldn't keep it in her pants while her boyfriend was away.

When we arrive at the safehouse, I lead Aurora inside and she's still as quiet as the grave.

I grab the duffel bag full of clothes and hand her a pair of basketball shorts and a T-shirt.

"Sorry, we didn't anticipate any women being in this safehouse," I apologize, but she just takes the clothes and goes into the bathroom downstairs, not saying a word.

I rub my hand across my face, cursing under my breath. This isn't how I thought I would spend my weekend, that's for sure.

I call Dante while she's in the bathroom, heading into the kitchen to see if there's a bottle of whiskey somewhere. Thank god, there is, and I pour myself a generous helping and knock it back while I wait for Dante to answer.

"Ricci," he barks.

"How's Francesca?" I ask instantly.

"She's sleeping now. Mia gave her a sedative," he says, and I let out a sigh of relief. "How's Aurora?"

"Almost catatonic," I say softly. "She's been through a lot."

"What's the plan?" he asks.

"Marco will be on the run. The hit wasn't sanctioned, and all of the Espositos will be on the lookout for him," I say. "The problem should take care of itself, but I need to keep Aurora safe in the meantime."

"Noted," Dante says easily. "Use the cash safe in the safe-house," he says. "There's about thirty grand in there."

"Thanks, *capo*," I say, and I mean it.

"No problem. I'll keep your sister safe."

I hang up the phone and Aurora comes out of the bathroom, the shirt and shorts hanging off of her.

She rubs her hands across her arms.

"Where should I sleep?" she asks meekly.

I gesture upstairs. "There's three bedrooms up there," I tell her. "Pick one."

She flinches a little at my tone and I feel like a real asshole. Sure, tonight has been stressful for me, but it's been a lot more stressful for her.

"I don't want to sleep alone," she says quietly, and I nod, pouring another glass of whiskey and offering it for her.

"I'll stay with you," I promise. "Until you fall asleep."

She looks up at me and throws back the whiskey in the glass.

"Thank you," she says quietly. "For everything."

I shake my head. "Thank you for keeping an eye on Francesca. I'm sorry it didn't go the way we wanted."

She puts the glass down on the table and turns, looking back at me as if expecting me to follow. I grab the duffel bag so that I can change into something more comfortable and follow her up the stairs. I head into the master bedroom, since there's a bathroom in there, and change into a T-shirt and a pair of sweats. Having my dress clothes off seems to make my chest feel less tight, at least.

When I come out, Aurora has climbed onto the bed,

getting up under the covers, and she's lying on her side, looking at me.

"Nico?" she asks softly when I sit down in the chair next to the bed. "Will you hold me? Just for a little while?"

I swallow hard, thinking I can't deny her such a simple request after everything she's been through.

I climb into bed with her and put my arms around her, drawing her close. She sighs and leans back against me, and I move my hips away from her ample ass, not wanting to embarrass her or myself.

"Goodnight, Aurora," I say, thinking that there's no way I'll be able to sleep, but I'm out almost as soon as my head hits the pillow.

5

AURORA

I wake up with Nico's arms wrapped around me, and it takes me a long moment to figure out where I am and what's going on. Then I remember last night, a flash across my memory of Bruno's face, and I gasp.

Nico murmurs something in his sleep and rocks against me, his morning erection pressing against my ass.

I swallow hard. My teenage self would be *living* right now, having Nico in bed with me, holding me, pressing up against me, but I don't know how to handle it.

I just don't want to think anymore. I don't want to see Bruno's dead body, think about the fact that he's just...gone.

I don't want to think about Marco's heavy breaths as he chased me through the woods, how I was only able to get rid of him by climbing over a rose bush which cut along my legs.

So, instead of thinking, I turn around and press my mouth against Nico's.

He wakes up with a start, putting his hands on my shoulders.

"Aurora?" he mumbles against my mouth.

"I don't want to think," I say, kissing down his throat. "Keep me from thinking so much," I plead, and I think he's going to push me away. Of course, he's going to push me away. He doesn't want me. No one wants me.

But instead, Nico moans low in the back of his throat and lifts my chin up with one hand, just like he did last night.

He kisses me hard and hungry, kisses *me* instead of the other way around, and my heart soars, my body heating up all over.

My hands trail down his back, scratching my acrylic nails down his bare flesh. He lost the T-shirt sometime in the night, and I'm grateful.

His chest is broad and tight and he pulls me closer, rolling his hips against me so that I can feel him hard and thick against my thigh.

I moan into his mouth and he pulls away, panting.

"Are you sure this is what you want, Aurora?" he asks me, searching my face with those sea-green eyes.

I can't speak, so I just nod eagerly, clutching at him, and he rolls over to cover my body with his own, kissing along my neck and collarbone before tearing down my shirt to get to my breasts.

They spill out of the ruined shirt and he latches around a nipple. My back arches and I cry out. I haven't been with a man since high school, since my one and only boyfriend. But he was just a stupid boy.

I've never been with a man like Nico.

He moves his tongue around my peaked nipple, and it sends heat down between my legs and I spread my thighs. He pulls his head up finally, after torturing me for a while, and pulls my shorts down and off, throwing them to the ground. He sits up on his knees and I can see his hardness through his sweats, see how long and thick he is and my eyes widen.

Is that even going to fit?

I hadn't had any trouble with my previous boyfriend, but he wasn't nearly as blessed as Nico.

He pushes down his sweats, freeing himself with a groan, and I think he's just going to slide into me but he pauses, cupping his hand against my sex.

I moan and rock my hips toward his hand and when he slips two fingers inside me, I gasp.

"So wet and ready for me," Nico murmurs, angling his fingers up, and I'm being vaulted toward an orgasm I never expected.

I've never actually had an orgasm that wasn't by myself. I've never experienced it during sex with a man, and I feel like I'm going to explode. Before I can fully reach my orgasm, though, Nico removes his fingers and I whine.

He chuckles. "Thought you might want the real thing, *principessa.*"

Before I can complain further, he guides himself into me, sliding in slowly, inch by inch, and I lose my breath, gasping.

He feels so good, stretching me out, and I babble something to that affect and Nico groans low in the back of his throat.

"You talk like that, *principessa,* and it's going to be over too soon."

I rock my hips against his frantically, wanting more friction, and Nico hisses and takes my hips in his hands forcefully. I think I might have fingerprint bruises there and the idea makes my head spin.

He begins to slide in and out of me, slowly at first, and then harder, licking his lips and then biting down on his lower lip as he looks down at where we're joined, his dark hair falling in his face.

This is like every dirty dream I've ever had, and I can't believe that it's really happening. Nico Andretti is inside me, and it's real.

He slides against a sensitive spot inside me and black spots bloom behind my closed eyelids when I come around him, clenching tight around his dick.

Nico groans an almost-growl deep in his chest and fucks me harder, through my orgasm, before spilling hot inside me.

"Shit," he curses, rolling his hips a few more times and making me squeak out in pleasure. "You're on the pill, right?"

My head still spinning, I nod. I am, although I'm not a hundred percent sure I've been taking it this week. I take it to help with my irregular periods, but since I'm not having sex, I don't think too much about it.

Nico sighs in relief and rolls off me with a long moan.

"That was something else, Aurora," he chuckles.

I blush all over, looking down at my ripped shirt. "You're telling me."

"Did it help?"

I stare at him blankly. "What?"

"You said you didn't want to think. Did it help?"

"I'm not thinking *anything*," I say, and Nico laughs, rubbing a hand over his face.

"Then it did work," he chuckles.

I have no idea what to do with myself now, so I stand up on shaky legs. "I think I'll take a shower," I mumble, and Nico nods, throwing a forearm over his eyes.

I stare at myself in the mirror for a long time, at the

marks that Nico left on my throat, the little red bruises on my hips. Had that really just happened?

Did I just sleep with Nico Andretti?

I take a deep breath and run the shower as hot as I can, standing under the spray. Luckily, I can't think about poor Bruno when I just had the best sex of my life with my best friend's older brother. I'm able to push it out of my mind.

I let the water run cold before I get out, and Nico's sitting up, shirtless, on the edge of the bed when I come out in a robe, my dark hair wet and cascading down my back. I haven't cut it since I was a teenager, and it's probably my only vanity.

Nico looks up at me and I bite my lip.

"What do we do now?"

Nico shrugs. "We wait. You like to play cards?"

I smile slightly. "Only if it's Texas Hold 'Em."

"A woman after my own heart," Nico jokes, but my heart skips a beat nonetheless.

I follow him when he heads to the kitchen and my stomach growls loudly.

"I'll make you something to eat first," Nico suggests, and I sit down at the table and watch him make scrambled eggs and toast with ham from the refrigerator. "Dante keeps this place stocked," he explains.

My mouth is watering at the smell, and I scarf down the eggs as Nico watches with a smile.

"You eat well," he says, but it doesn't sound like a criticism like it does when other people say it.

"I know, right? You can tell," I say, looking down at my belly roll as I sit down.

Nico frowns. "Eating well is an attractive quality in a woman."

"It is?" I ask incredulously, and he nods.

"You're very beautiful, Aurora. You should know that," he says quietly, and heat rushes through me, making my cheeks red.

"Thank you," I mumble, not knowing exactly what to say. It's not like Nico's going to *be* with me now. I'm not stupid enough to think that. But it means something that we slept together, right? It means that he's at least attracted to me, and that's something.

It means a lot, honestly, and I think that being on the run might not be so bad after all, especially when Nico laughs so hard at one of my jokes that he nearly snorts coffee out of his nose.

"You're funny," he says, almost accusatory, and I laugh.

"Is that a compliment?"

"I guess so," he says in a low tone, shoveling more eggs onto my plate. I push it away from me, frowning.

"I can't eat another bite," I say.

Nico looks around outside after breakfast, while I'm loading the dishwasher. I can't help but think that this is all rather domestic, and that I could get used to this.

I could get used to being with Nico Andretti like this, but it isn't going to last forever. I need to remember that.

6

NICO

I call Dante while I'm checking the perimeter of the safe house.

"Any news?" I ask as soon as he picks up.

"Not yet," he answers. "Angelo swears he spotted Marco running down the highway, but he couldn't catch up with him after the party, so who knows."

"Angelo doesn't drink," I say with a frown. "Why wouldn't you believe him?"

Dante sighs. "I don't know, it was dark, so I'm taking it with a pinch of salt, I guess."

I hum in response. I suppose he is right, there were some pretty dark areas around there, so unless it was a very lit area, who knows who Angelo saw.

"I'm going to move safehouses. Marco's men might know where this one is," I say.

"Yeah, we worked together a few years ago," Dante agrees. "Best to set up for a while at the one upstate."

I groan, "I hate upstate."

Dante laughs. "It's not a vacation, Nico. How's the girl? Francesca's been asking about her."

"She's...all right," I hedge, not wanting Francesca to know that we hooked up. "How's my annoying little sister?"

"Annoying," Dante answers jokingly. "Nah, she's been okay. Just worried about you and her friend."

"Do you think that Marco will come after her?" I ask.

"No. I think he's worried about Aurora, honestly, and he might be on your tail. I'm sure he's managed to get a car by now."

"Fuck," I curse. "All right, I'll take Aurora and leave by tonight."

"Make sure you ditch your phone. Use one of the burners."

"Noted."

I break the phone with my hands and leave it in the dirt outside before walking back into the house. Aurora sits at the table, dressed now in a pair of biking shorts that show off her ass and a T-shirt that she's got tied up above her belly button.

I do my best not to look her up and down, but damn, it's hard.

"Listen, Aurora," I start, planning to tell her that I'm going to take her to a new safehouse, but she bites her lip and looks away.

"I understand," she says quickly, and I blink at her.

"Understand what?"

"I understand that this can't happen again," she mumbles.

"What—" I freeze, finally understanding. She means the sex. "You don't want it to happen again?"

She looks up at me, her bottom lip still caught between her teeth. "I mean, not if you don't," she manages.

I smirk at her. "So, I get whatever I want?"

"Pretty much, yeah," she agrees, and I bark out a laugh, leaning over to kiss her on her nose.

"Well then, I guess we'll see, *principessa.*" I pause and she just looks up at me with a blush spreading across her face. "We're going upstate to another safehouse," I tell her.

Aurora's brows draw together. "Why? Is something wrong? Francesca—"

I shake my head quickly. "She's fine," I say. "Everything's fine, but we aren't sure how safe this place is. Dante's had it for a while and Marco might know where it is."

Aurora looks terrified, and I put my hand on her shoulder.

"You're not going to let anything happen to me," she says slowly in a quiet voice.

I smile at her. "That's right, *principessa.* I'm not." And I mean it.

She looks around at the kitchen. "I don't have anything to pack," she says, and I chuckle a little, grabbing the duffel bag, which has a needle and thread, some gauze, more clothes, and the quarter-empty bottle of whiskey I'd found in the cabinet.

"We're already packed," I tell her, and head out to the car. She follows after taking a bathroom break and she's a lot more obedient than Francesca would have been in the same situation. She buckles her seatbelt and sits quietly as we take off. She doesn't ask too many questions or chatter too much.

I'm beginning to think this might be a mini vacation instead of a difficult situation where I feel stuck.

Aurora is good company and *definitely* eye candy. I don't know why I haven't noticed before that she's exactly my type. I'm not against starting a physical relationship with her, at least as long as Francesca doesn't know.

Physical being the operative word. I don't get close to people, nature of the job, and especially not to women. Being in love is a weakness, and I've told Dante that over and over. Anyone who gets ahold of Mia will *own* him, and I don't want that for my own life.

I don't want anyone to own me just by virtue of taking someone I love, and I've already got enough trouble with Francesca and my mother, who hasn't been well for some time.

I sigh, not wanting to think about my family, and Aurora looks at me sideways. I want to get as much of this drive done as I can before nightfall, so I keep my eyes on the road.

"What are you thinking about?" Aurora asks, and I don't know why I tell her the truth. Maybe because she's the only person I'll be around for the next week or so, maybe because we slept together last night. Maybe because she's just easy to talk to.

"My mother," I say, and Aurora hums.

"I think about my mother a lot," she says quietly.

I glance over at her. "Are you and your mother close?"

She barks out a bitter laugh. "She left when I was seven," she says. "Chose drugs over me and my dad."

"Shit. I'm sorry."

Aurora shrugs. "It is what it is."

"My father died when I was twelve," I tell her.

Aurora nods. "Yeah, Francesca says she doesn't really remember him."

Francesca. I almost forget, spending time with Aurora, that she's my little sister's best friend. I'm only about six years older than her, but it seems like a lifetime given that Francesca doesn't exactly act like she's twenty-seven years old. More like seventeen.

"It's better to have a dead parent than one who doesn't

care about you, I guess," I mumble, not really sure how to respond.

Aurora laughs softly. "I've never heard it put quite that way before, but I guess you're right." She pauses. "But I'd never want to be without my father. Even if sometimes he is not as present as I'd like, he's all I have left."

"Daddy's little girl?" I ask with a smirk, and she smiles.

"Yeah, you could say that," she says. "He's been sick and I'm worried about him."

She bites at her bottom lip, a nervous gesture.

"I'll have someone check on him, if it'll make you feel better," I offer, and she gives me a grateful smile.

"It would make me feel better."

"Consider it done," I tell her, and then someone pulls out onto the road behind us. I don't think much of it at first, but when I take the next exit, they take it, too. I frown.

"What's wrong?" she asks.

"I don't know," I say honestly. "But I need you to get down."

"What do you mean, get down?" she asks, staring at me blankly, and I grab the back of her head and push her down into my lap.

"Someone's tailing us," I hiss. "So, stay down."

Aurora makes a squeak of surprise but stays down.

I look in the rearview mirror, and sure enough, bullets ring out, one shattering the back glass.

"Fuck!" I swing the car sideways, right in front of an ongoing semi. If this asshole wants to play chicken, we'll play chicken.

The semi begins to lay down on the horn and I speed up, getting so close that my heart is pounding in my ears and I can see the pale, scared look on the trucker's face before I yank the steering wheel to the right, going back into the lane. I look back behind me and the other car, an old Ford, has gone off road. They're still trying to catch up. Aurora's still down, head on my lap, shattered glass in her hair, but I'm only focused on one thing – getting us out of this alive.

I swerve off-road and drive through some farmland to get back on the main road, close to downtown. I weave in and out of traffic, running red lights until I finally make it to the nearest parking garage that Dante owns.

I swing the car inside and Aurora is hyperventilating again, so I tug her up gently when we park.

"It's all right. We're all right," I tell her, breathing hard myself.

"What do we do?" she asks, panicked, shaking the glass out of her hair. I pick a few pieces out, being careful not to cut her face.

"We're going to steal a car," I say firmly, and get out. She follows me after a dazed moment as I hotwire an old pickup truck and then switch the plates with another car's.

Aurora hops up in the truck and I grab the duffel bag out of my car, cursing.

I hate to leave the car behind, but I can always ask Dante to have someone pick it up and take it home for me. I have all I need. Her and the thirty grand from the safe in the duffel bag.

I'm not exactly getting paid for this job, but Dante will let me handle expenses. Though I'm stealing a car now, I know I'll probably have to buy another one along the way, but if that's what we need to keep her safe, so be it.

There are perks to working for your best friend.

Aurora keeps looking at me as I pull out onto the street again, and when we're back on the highway, she's still breathing hard.

"What?" I ask her, glancing over at her and then back at the road.

"That was...really hot," she says in a sultry voice. "How do you feel about road head?"

I bark out a laugh. "You're really something, *principessa*," I murmur, and then lower her head into my lap for entirely different reasons.

7

AURORA

Nico's still wearing a pair of sweats and I tug them down with one hand, freeing him. He bobs up around my mouth, already half-hard, and he groans as I put my fingers around him, circling his base.

I'm not all that experienced with sex, but I've given head to my ex-boyfriend about a hundred times. He had preferred it to sex, after all.

It occurs to me now that my ex was a real asshole, but I didn't realize that at the time.

I feel more comfortable doing this with Nico, so I wrap my lips around him, taking him into my mouth and sucking gently.

Nico thrusts up beneath me, one hand on the wheel and one in my hair. There's probably still glass in my hair, but I don't care. I'm already hot and wet between my legs from watching him so deftly handle such a dangerous situation.

Nico is such a *man*, and it's only becoming more and more clear that he's perfect the more time I spend with him. I feel validated in my huge crush on him.

He thrusts up into my mouth again, gagging me slightly,

and when I choke around him, he lets out this low groan, tugging my hair.

"I'm close," he grunts, and I hollow my cheeks, sucking harder and letting myself go limp, letting him guide me.

He pulses on my tongue, letting out a low moan as he fucks into my mouth, and then he spills down my throat. I swallow easily, smiling as I come up off him, and throwing my hair back over my shoulder.

"Jesus Christ," Nico says shakily, and I realize we're driving down a country road going about twenty miles an hour.

I giggle, unable to help myself, and Nico looks over at me, licking his lips. "Too bad I can't return the favor."

"You can when we get there," I croon, feeling a lot more confident and wanton than I ever have before.

"Bet on it," Nico says with a grin, pulling off onto another country road.

I'm dozing against the window by the time we arrive at the safehouse, and Nico wakes me up by opening my door and shaking me gently.

"We're here, *principessa*," he says softly, and I take his hand and climb out of the truck with a yawn.

He's grabbed the duffel bag and heads inside, using one of the many keys on his keyring. It's a smaller house than the other one, off by itself, clearly somewhere upstate even though I've slept the last leg of the drive.

It looks to be just one bedroom, and it's only one story. It's smaller even than my father's house, which is saying something.

"I know it's small," Nico says, and I shake my head.

"Better than getting killed," I comment, and Nico laughs.

"Fair enough. There's only one bed."

I grin. "Fine with me. Don't you owe me one?" I ask,

stripping off the man's T-shirt that I'm wearing and heading toward the little bedroom.

Nico groans and curses under his breath, dropping the duffel bag and sweeping me up into his arms. I gasp. It's so hot the way he can pick me up so easily, carry me to the bedroom, his biceps and forearms bulging. He's strong, to be able to carry someone like me.

"You're kind of a bad girl, *principessa*," he murmurs, tossing me onto the bed, his eyes on my bouncing breasts.

He tugs off the biking shorts I'm wearing, biting at the edge of my ass until I squeak and laugh. I feel giddy, happier than I have in a really long time, despite the fact that I've been in terrible danger throughout this whole trip.

"Not as bad as you," I tease, and then I can't speak anymore because Nico pushes his face against my sex, lapping at my clitoris lazily and moving to slide two fingers inside me. He arches them up, just like he knows I like, and I can't stop myself from crying out his name.

"You're so tight around me, bad girl," he teases. "Love having something stretch you out, don't you?"

"Yes," I breathe. "Want more."

"Of course you do," he mutters, his tone almost harsh, and then he latches onto my clit, sucking hard, and pleasure begins to build in my lower stomach.

I'm almost there, and he's pumping his fingers in and out of me when I come, gasping in deep breaths and calling out his name. Nico pulls away from me, breathing in deeply like he's been holding his breath and moving his fingers out of me before lining up. He taps one of my hips while I'm still gasping.

"Turn over," he demands. "Want to see that ass of yours jiggling against me."

I do as he says immediately, turning over and getting up

on all fours, spreading my thighs. He pushes into me almost instantly, and I moan loud and long.

He's stretching me out from a whole other angle now, and I can't stop moaning. Nico grunts, thrusting forward, and I brace myself on the headboard. It slams against the wall as he fucks me, and I'm glad we don't have any neighbors because they certainly would have heard us.

"Fuck me," I gasp. "Fuck me hard, Nico."

"Don't have to ask me twice," he groans, and slams his hips against my ass, his balls hitting against my clit until I come again, clenching around him.

He fucks me through my orgasm and keeps going, long after I think he's done, finally pulling out and spilling all over my ass and lower back.

I whine a little, wanting him to come inside, but I don't complain when he takes off his shirt and cleans me off. Still panting, he stands up and undresses all the way, padding to the bathroom. I stare after him, having lost my breath, and then he turns around and tilts his head. He makes a come-hither gesture with his fingers, and I climb off the bed to join him, unable to stop grinning.

In the shower, I can see more of him than I ever have, the light dusting of hair on his chest and belly, his dick hanging heavy between his legs. I try not to stare, looking up at his face instead, but that's not better.

He's just so *gorgeous* that it makes me nervous. I know that he's seen me naked already, that he's just been inside me, for god's sake, but I still feel self-conscious somehow. I cover my belly with my hands but Nico doesn't seem to notice, leaning down and kissing my nose, groaning under the hot water. He moves aside to let me wet my hair and then next thing I know, he's got his hands in my hair, lathering it up with shampoo. My hair is long enough to graze my ass, and he washes all of it, massaging my scalp.

"You're so pretty," he mumbles as I tilt my head back to rinse my hair, and I blink, looking at him upside down.

"You are," I say, and he laughs.

"I'm pretty?"

"Very," I assure him, and Nico just chuckles again, shaking his head.

"Thanks, I guess. You're not very good at accepting compliments."

"Neither are you."

"So says you. I'm great at accepting compliments," he argues. "Yours was just a weird one. I usually get that I'm handsome."

"You *are* handsome," I agree.

"Thank you," he says with a smirk. "I know."

I roll my eyes but I'm smiling.

"No ego there."

"Plenty of ego," he says easily, and I laugh in response.

Nico finishes first and gets out of the shower, putting on a robe. I do the same after finishing conditioning my long hair. It's dark outside when I come out to the terrace, watching Nico with a cigarette in his mouth.

"You smoke?" I ask.

He turns his head to look at me. "Do you?" he asks.

I shake my head. "Not since high school." He laughs and shakes his head. "I think I'm addicted to the feel of a cigarette in my mouth, but I hardly ever light it. It's not a healthy habit and I'm trying hard to quit for good. You had the right idea."

I can't help but look Nico up and down. I know that he doesn't want me past this physical relationship, but I'm enjoying it.

Yes, I've got feelings for him, but at the same time, I understand that this is all I can get.

Girls like me don't get the guy forever. They get the guy for a little while.

I can deal with that. Right?

8

NICO

"That's it," Aurora says. "It's official."

I look up from my coffee. She's standing in front of the refrigerator, wearing one of my T-shirts, the curve of her ass hanging out, and I stare unabashedly at it.

After all, we're kind of playing house right now, so I'm allowed, right?

This will all change when we get back home, but for now....

"Stop looking at my ass and listen to me," she says, frustrated, and I laugh.

"Okay, *principessa.* What's wrong?"

"We're officially out of all food products," she says with a huff. "You've got to make a supply run."

"Really? We're out of *everything*?"

"It wasn't as well stocked as the other place," she argues, and I stand up and stand behind her, looking into the fridge.

She's right, there's nothing in there but condiments.

"We can't eat ketchup for dinner," I say. "I guess we used the last of the eggs this morning?"

"Your fault, you make the best eggs," she grumbles, and I lean down and kiss the crown of her head.

"I'll go out and get more supplies before dinner. Don't worry."

Aurora looks up at me. "You take such good care of me."

She looks cute, and for the first time, I notice that there's freckles marching across her nose. It makes my heart clench, and I look away.

It's been four days since we got to the new safehouse, four days since the car chase, and I think things are fairly safe. Marco doesn't know where we are, even though he'd tailed us from the first safehouse.

"Everything is going to be fine," I tell her as she bites her lip, looking into the fridge.

She smiles, turning to me, and I put my hands on her hips. "I know it is," she says gently.

"You just hunker down and I'll be back in a bit," I tell her. "Any special requests?"

"Bread and peanut butter," she says eagerly. "I miss peanut butter sandwiches."

I laugh. "Fair enough. What about chocolate?"

"Nutella," she says.

"A fair point," I muse, and scribble it down on a nearby notepad along with beer and other supplies we might need.

She waves to me at the door and my breath hitches in my chest. What if this is the last time I see her? What if Marco or his men are hiding out somewhere, biding their time, waiting for me to leave the house?

I pause outside the door. "Get dressed," I bark. "You're coming with me."

She blinks at me. "I'm *what*?"

"You're coming with me," I tell her, walking back inside. "We'll get you some real clothes, too, but for now, wear these sweats and a hoodie, put all your hair under a cap."

"That's a lot of hair," she muses, but does as I say without complaint. She looks cute, all undercover, and I kiss her nose again before taking her by the hand and leading her to the car.

I don't feel safe going to the corner store, thinking that somewhere in public will be better, so I go to a big box store further up in the small town that we're staying in.

"Why did you want me to come with you?" she asks, something odd in her tone.

"Maybe I'd miss you," I mumble.

"Really?" she asks with a grin.

"No," I confess, laughing. "I just was worried that Marco might have someone waiting outside. I want you with me so that I can protect you."

"Of course," she mutters, and for a moment, I think she's actually upset with me, but then she smiles and it's all over.

Aurora really takes most things in stride, and I'm realizing that she's even more different than I thought from Francesca.

We walk inside and she grabs a cart, pushing it as I trail behind her. We rack up a truly ridiculous amount of groceries.

Aurora also picks out some clothes, smiling a little and not showing me a few of her purchases, and I'm just hoping they're lingerie based.

The total comes to almost five hundred dollars' worth, including her clothes, and we load it all into the car. There's no one suspicious trailing around, and no one bats an eye at us.

Maybe I'm being a little paranoid, but you can't be too careful when someone is trying to kill you, right?

When we get back home, I unload the groceries and she goes upstairs to change, coming back down in a little string bikini.

I stare at her for a long moment, my dick jumping in my sweats, and she rubs her hand along her belly as if trying to hide it.

"It's too much, isn't it?"

I nod slowly. "It's definitely too much if anyone else were to see you in it," I growl, walking toward her and grabbing at her ass.

She squeals and darts away from me toward the back door. "Well, I wanted to make good use of the pool."

Ah, the pool.

She's always loved the pool at our house, spending hours out there with Francesca, both of them getting tan over the summers.

"Funny that you think you're going to keep that on in the pool with me around," I mutter.

She laughs and runs toward the pool, diving into the deep end in a cannonball.

I laugh at her and take off my clothes entirely, skinny dipping and chasing her across the pool as if I'm a shark.

It's all fun and games until I catch her and untie her top, letting it float away as I put my mouth around one nipple, and then the next. She writhes under the water, wrapping her legs around my waist and I thrust against her.

Pool sex isn't all it's cracked up to be, but it's nice just making out with her, dry humping like a couple of teenagers. I haven't spent this much time with a woman in a long time, it's mostly just been one to three night stands.

So, this amount of time is unusual, but I have to admit it's kind of nice to get to know her body, for her to get to know mine. Getting to know each other's triggers is part of the fun, really.

She unwraps herself from around me and climbs up out of the pool, lying down on the ground on a beach towel that she bought.

"It's so nice out today," she comments, and I grunt, heaving myself out of the pool and crawling toward her. She's still topless and I can't stop staring at her ample breasts.

When I get closer, I untie one side of her bottoms and lay her bare beneath me. I lie on my shoulder next to her, playing idly between her lower lips, running my thumb across her clit.

She gasps, arching her back and spreading her thighs, her nipples peaking toward the sky.

"*Principessa,*" I murmur. "What do you want?"

"Want you to make me come," she whines, and heat rushes through my body. I want to spear into her right now, I'm hard as diamond against her thigh, but part of the fun of being with Aurora is how sensitive she is, how easily I can make her come.

I slip my fingers through her heat, sliding a couple into her, and she moans out my name.

I can't wait anymore, can't make her come because my balls are aching and I keep rolling my hips against her. So, I line up, covering her body with my own, my chest scraping across her nipples, and slide into her. I fuck her hard and rough, not bothering to do anything but chase my own orgasm, and after teasing her for a while, she's so hot and slick I could almost slide out of her.

She clenches around me when she does come and claws her nails down my back. The acrylic bites into my flesh and I hiss, leaning down to bite at her neck. I've always loved marking my lovers, but Aurora takes the bites so well, moans at every single one.

I fuck her through her orgasm before spilling inside her, and Aurora sighs happily when I collapse against her, holding myself up by my forearms.

"It's such a nice day," she says again, and I laugh, kissing along the side of her face.

"Now, how about I cook some of those expensive groceries we bought?" I ask her.

"Perfect," she says, grinning at me, and my heart lurches into my throat for reasons I can't explain.

I think I need to be careful with Aurora Costa.

9

AURORA

I sit at the table and watch Nico cooking dinner.

"I never learned to cook," I admit. "My father did all the cooking."

"Can't boil water?" he asks me teasingly.

I huff. "I can make boxed stuff," I argue.

He groans. "Your Italian ancestors must be rolling around in their graves when you say that."

I laugh. "Maybe."

Nico looks around at my clothes strewn across the living room.

"You don't clean, either?"

I pout. "I do, just haven't gotten around to it." I smile. "My legs still don't work."

He grins. "You're lucky you're cute." He pauses. "I do want you to pack up all your things, keep it in one of those duffels. You never know when we're going to have to bug out of here."

"Do you think he's still looking for us?"

"I need to call Dante," he says, and leaves the burner on. "Watch that for me. Just stir every few moments."

I can hear him on the phone out on the terrace, can see the smoke billowing out of his nostrils.

"Any news?" he asks, and then pauses while Dante answers.

I try not to listen because it makes me anxious, focusing instead on stirring the tomato sauce that Nico has been working on. It smells delicious, like onions and garlic.

He got so many fresh ingredients. I would have just gotten some corndogs and chicken nuggets, so I'm glad I'm stuck with a chef.

Nico walks back inside, his face blank.

"What's up?" I ask nervously, stepping back from the stove.

He doesn't answer right away, instead straining the pasta into a colander.

"Everything's okay," he assures me, but he doesn't sound like everything is really okay.

"Nico," I say in a warning tone. "Don't lie to me."

He looks up at me with a sigh. "They haven't found Marco yet. Angelo and Dante have been working together to find him, but no news yet. They found his car abandoned nearby the old safehouse. He was the one following us."

I guess I'd known that much, but it still makes my face go pale.

"He doesn't know where this one is," I say flatly, hoping that's true.

"He doesn't," Nico assures me, pouring the sauce over the pasta and sitting it on the table. I spoon myself out a little and take a piece of garlic bread.

Nico's truly an amazing cook, but it doesn't matter because everything tastes like cardboard to me. I'm stressed and worried, and I just know I'm going to have nightmares again tonight.

I've had them every night since we began staying in the safehouses, waking up sweaty and running to the bathroom so I wouldn't wake up Nico.

I find myself trembling a little as I reach for another slice of garlic bread, and Nico grabs my hand.

"Aurora," he says firmly. "I'm not going to let anything happen to you."

I look into his sea-green eyes and I believe him, whole-heartedly, my breathing and heart rate slowing down.

Nico wouldn't lie to me. Not about this.

We finish dinner, chatting idly about the pool and the things we'd bought. Again, it feels awfully domestic and I know that I'm going to miss this when we're safe again.

Now that I think about it, how do I even know that Nico doesn't have a girl waiting for him at home, worried about him.

"Nico," I say, meaning to ask him, and he looks up at me. "Do you..." But I can't finish that sentence. What if he says no? What if he says yes? I shake my head. "Never mind."

"What is it, *principessa?*" he asks, and I realize I need an answer anyway.

"I just wanted to know if you have a girlfriend," I say meekly, feeling stupid and small.

Nico laughs loud and open. "Absolutely not."

I look at him curiously. "Really? You don't?"

"You know about my reputation, Aurora. You know that I don't do relationships."

I hum. "Doesn't mean you don't have a girl who'd get mad if she knew you said that," I tease, but I'm serious. I want to know if he's seeing anyone else.

"Maybe," he agrees, grinning. "But I don't. Not right now." He looks at me for a long moment. "What about you? Do you have someone at home?"

"Don't you think Francesca would have told you about it?"

He shrugs. "She keeps your secrets."

"She does? News to me," I mutter, and Nico is still staring at me.

"You didn't answer my question."

"You really think I have a boyfriend? Me?"

"Why wouldn't you? Looking the way you do," he says, sounding exasperated.

"I don't," I say simply. "Not in a really long time."

Nico's still staring at me intently. "Good," he mutters.

"Why do you ask, Mr. Andretti?" I ask in a teasing tone. "Would you be jealous?"

"Very," he admits, looking away for a moment as if embarrassed. "Guess I'm territorial."

"Me too," I admit. "That's why I wanted to know."

"Well, there's only you, *principessa*," he says softly, and my heart skips a few beats. "At least for now."

I fight a frown. *For now.*

I know that this can't last forever. I know that he's going to ditch me the first chance he can, that he's been stuck with me all this time. I know that he probably can't wait to get rid of me.

"I'm not feeling too well," I say. "Think I'll skip dessert."

Nico frowns. "But I bought your weird birthday cake ice cream."

I smile at him. "Maybe tomorrow."

I walk over to the bedroom, expecting to fall asleep easily, but I toss and turn until Nico comes to bed, wrapping me up in his arms. I've changed into a little nightie that I picked up at the store, and his fingers trail along the lace.

He hums against my hair, kissing the crown of my head, and then it's easy to fall asleep, cradled in his arms.

❧

NICO STANDS *at the end of the bed, staring at me, the shadows in the dark room covering his face so that I can't quite see him.*

"What are you doing up?" I ask, yawning, stretching and sitting up. "Why aren't you in bed?"

"Couldn't sleep," he mutters, and there's something wrong with his voice, something liquid in his throat.

"Nico?" I call, suddenly afraid, suddenly cold all over, and I rub my hands along my arms to try and warm up. Instead, goosebumps pop out along my flesh.

"Go back to sleep. It'll be easier that way," he says, stepping closer to me, and when I look up into his face, the moonlight shines right on it.

Marco's intense blue eyes look down at me instead of Nico's sea green ones, but that's not even the worst part. The worst part is that his face has a line of blood trailing from his forehead, just like Bruno's, blood filling one blue eye.

"Just close your eyes," he says, his voice still liquid with all the blood. "It'll be over soon."

I wake up screaming bloody murder, and this time I can't hide it from Nico because he has to put his arms around me just to calm me down.

I'm trembling all over.

"What happened? *Principessa*, what's wrong?" he asks.

"A dream," I breathe, gasping for air. "Bad dream."

He frowns, looking at me. "Have you been having these bad dreams the whole time?"

I nod slowly, looking up at him with what have to be wide, scared eyes.

"You never woke me up," he accuses.

"I didn't want to bother you," I whisper.

Nico pulls me closer, and I bury my face in his chest. "You're never a bother to me," he says fiercely.

"I'm always upset, always crying," I sob against his chest. "You always have to take care of me. I didn't want you to have to all the time."

I don't tell him that I don't want to be a burden, that I want to be fun and light and for him to fall in love with me, but that's all true, too.

I'm choking on my own sobs and Nico pulls away, looking down into my face.

"Look at me, *principessa*," he commands, and I won't do it, so he takes one hand and cups my chin, forcing me to look at him like he did the night my whole life changed. "You're safe. I've got you," he promises.

I take in a deep breath through my nostrils to calm down, blowing out through my mouth. Nico breathes slowly with me, and eventually, I begin to calm down and stop shaking. Nico draws me back into his arms and I feel exhausted, like I haven't slept in days, and I guess it's from all the nightmares.

"Wake me up any time you have a bad dream," he murmurs. "I'm here to keep you safe, even from your own memories."

My heart aches at his sweet words, and I nuzzle up against his chest. I think I'll never be able to get to sleep, but between his strong arms, broad chest, and the sound of his heartbeat, I manage to drift off easily.

10

NICO

It's becoming more and more clear to me that Marco isn't going to get himself caught, and that I'm going to have to go after him. I tell myself it's because I don't want to be stuck in safehouses or looking over my shoulder when I get home, but I know, deep down, that it's not that.

I want to kill him myself for what he's done to Aurora. He's broken her in many ways, and she seems dimmer after those nightmares.

He's given a bright young girl something to be afraid of, and I hate him for it.

It's not because I have feelings for Aurora. That's not possible. I don't get feelings for women, but I do like to protect them. She's my little sister's best friend, so of course I want to protect her. Francesca would be lost without her, honestly.

They're like sisters.

When Aurora is still sleeping, I get up and pack all our things, putting away all her clothes and packing some snacks for us as well as the first aid kit that came in the original duffel bag. I want us to have a way out if we need it.

I call Dante and he picks up on the fourth ring.

"Why do you call me so early?" he groans.

"I haven't heard from you in two days," I snap.

I can all but hear Dante's scowl. "Well, there hasn't been much to say," he says. "They still haven't caught Marco. There's been no sign of him since we found the car."

"Well, we need to figure it out," I say, sighing. "I can't be stuck here forever."

"She can come here," Dante offers. "Stay with me and Mia."

I haven't thought of that. I could take Aurora home, and have her stay with Dante, Mia, and Francesca. I don't have to do this on my own.

But I look over at her, sleeping peacefully in bed, her fingers curled around my pillow, and I can't bring myself to tell Dante that I'll do it.

"There's no sign of him at all?" I ask, changing the subject.

"Nothing," he responds. "I've got people staked out all over the Esposito place and close as I can get to the Barones."

"They're protecting him?"

"Not officially," Dante sighs. "But yeah, they're going to protect their own, keep him from getting caught, most likely."

I curse under my breath. "So, in the meantime, we just have to wait it out?"

"Like I said, just bring her here," Dante says, sounding exasperated.

"I've got this," I say, even though I'm not that confident that I do.

"What's the deal, Nico? Do you like her or something?"

I scoff. "Don't be ridiculous. I'm just stuck with her, that's all."

I hang up the phone and start to make breakfast, but Aurora doesn't come out into the kitchen for a long time. When she does, she just grabs her plate and goes back into the bedroom, closing the door.

I stand at the closed door for a long time, looking at the doorknob but not turning it. Is she still upset about last night, about the dream she had? She wouldn't tell me about it, only told me that it was awful, full of memories from that night.

We've been at the new safehouse for six days now, and I'm getting antsy. I don't want Marco to trail us here and I keep thinking that he might.

I put my hand on the doorknob and open it and Aurora is lying down, the plate barely touched on the nightstand next to her. She's staring at the ceiling.

"I'm sorry that you have to be stuck with me," she says softly.

"Fuck." She heard that? "That's not what I meant, Aurora..." I trail off. What else could I have possibly meant? I sounded like an asshole.

"Why don't you just take me home?" she asks. "My father still has connections. He can call in some favors..."

I sit down on the edge of the bed, looking right at her.

"I want to see this through, Aurora."

"Why? You don't have to," she says stubbornly, and pulls away when I put a hand on her calf.

"I want to," I insist, and she scoffs, rolling over onto her side.

"You don't have to pretend with me, Nico. I know what this is."

"Do you?" I ask, getting a little angry. "Because I sure fucking don't."

"You're just having your fun," she says flatly. "And when we get back home, this will all be over."

"You'll be safe," I say, not wanting to get roped into a "what are we" conversation.

"Yeah," she says. "I'll be safe. I'll sleep on the couch tonight," she says, and stands up to go and empty her still full plate into the trash.

"Fuck," I curse again, running a hand through my hair, as she walks out onto the terrace where the pool is. She clearly needs some space and I'm going to give it to her.

I go out to the car briefly to get my guns out from under the seat of the truck and I start cleaning them in the living room. I might as well, since it's not like Aurora's going to talk to me anytime soon.

But really, what do I expect? She heard me say that I'm stuck with her. Anyone's feelings would be hurt. I need to apologize. She shouldn't have to hurt because I was callous with my words.

I'm not so good at apologies, though, especially when it comes to women. I groan and put down my guns after about half an hour, going outside to see Aurora sunbathing in her bikini in a pair of sunglasses.

My eyes rove over her body but I make myself focus on her face.

I sit next to her on the ground and she doesn't move away, so I'm a little encouraged.

"Aurora," I call, and she tilts her head slightly and I guess she's looking at me. I can't really tell because of the dark sunglasses. "I'm sorry."

"Sorry for what?" she asks flippantly.

"You know what," I mumble, but apparently, she's going

to make me say it. "I'm sorry for what you heard me say on the phone. I didn't mean it."

"Didn't you?"

"Dante offered for you to stay with him and Mia," I say quietly. "I said I wanted to stay with you, instead."

"Why?" she asks, sitting up and frowning. "Why would you want to stay when you could be rid of me?"

"I...I don't *want* to be rid of you, Aurora." I say hesitantly, stumbling over my words. "I'm not really good at this whole...talking things out."

"I need a little more than that," she says dryly.

"I like being here with you," I say finally, and it feels like it takes a lot out of me to say that. "I've enjoyed spending time with you."

"And?"

"And *what?*" I groan.

"And you want to protect me," she says.

"I want to protect you," I agree. "That's what I've done, this whole time. Right?"

"Right," she says, smiling just a little. "And part of you likes being stuck with me."

"I wouldn't go that far," I mutter, but I'm smiling as she climbs into my lap, my heart rate slowing. I don't like her being mad at me, it makes my heart race and makes me feel like shit, guilt hot at the back of my head.

"You like me, Mr. Andretti," she teases, and begins to kiss my neck.

Before I flip her over and start biting the back of her neck, I feel my cheeks flush, and I'm not much of a blusher.

She's not able to talk much after that, thank God.

IT TAKES two weeks to run out of supplies, and there's still no word about Marco. I'm getting more and more nervous that he's out there somewhere, biding his time. He would have had to get a new car, and that would have maybe taken a few days, seeing as he's a wanted man, but too much time has passed with no word.

The man isn't a ghost, for god's sake. He's Marco Barone, and he's a hothead. He should be making waves by now.

I talk to Dante every day, and eventually, to Francesca.

"Let me talk to Aurora," she demands.

"Good to hear from you too, sis," I drawl.

"Put her on the phone," she demands again, and I sigh.

"She's sleeping," I tell her.

"You better be taking care of her," she barks.

"I'm fine," I say flatly. "Thanks for asking."

"I *know* you're fine, you're too stubborn to die, but Aurora... she witnessed something really fucked up, Nico. You have to keep an eye on her."

"I am," I say, looking out to the pool where Aurora is sitting at the edge, dipping her toes in the water. My eyes are very much on her and that bikini I've untied with my teeth about a dozen times now.

"Have her call me back when she gets up," Francesca insists.

"All right, all right. You doing okay?" I ask her, genuinely wanting to know.

"I'm fine," she says. "Like you, too stubborn to die."

I snort out a laugh. "Fair enough."

I hang up the phone and walk over to Aurora, sitting next to her at the pool.

"Francesca wants you to call her," I tell her, and Aurora looks at me, her eyes lighting up.

"Can I?" she asks, as if she needs my permission, and I smile and nod.

"Just call Dante's number, ask for her," I tell her, and she bounces up and runs toward the lawn chair I've left my phone on.

She's way too cute, and I shouldn't be thinking about that. I shouldn't be smiling at her as she bounces into the kitchen.

I shouldn't be looking at her this way at all, but what else do I have to do?

Like I said to Dante, I *am* stuck with her, even if I don't mind it so much anymore.

11

AURORA

"Francesca?" I ask when Dante puts her on the phone.

"Aurora! God, it's so good to hear your voice," Francesca says, almost in a high-pitched squeal.

I wince and move the phone from my face, laughing a little. "It has been a while," I say.

"Are you dying having to hang out with my boring, stupid brother all this time?" she asks.

I think about the night before, Nico biting my neck as he thrust into me, and I blush. "He's not so bad."

Francesca scoffs. "You don't have to lie to me. All he talks about is pussy and crime. It's annoying."

I swallow hard at her words. Nico hasn't said anything to me about other women, but I know his reputation. Is it possible that he's still in contact with some of these women? Surely not, right?

"Does he have a girlfriend?" I ask, looking around for Nico. He's trailed inside, so I can speak freely.

Francesca snorts. "A girlfriend? Are you crazy? Nico wouldn't be caught dead in any kind of real commitment."

"Ah," I say dumbly, not knowing how to respond. I don't want Francesca to know that Nico and I have been hooking up. It's just...weird. Especially when I don't know where we stand. Or better yet, I do know, but I don't really want to dwell on the fact that this is just all happening in this bubble in time and space. That all of this will end just as soon as we get in the car to get back to our lives. To reality.

"He's got about a dozen girlfriends, I guess, if you want to think of one-night stands as girlfriends," Francesca says.

I hate listening to her talk about Nico like this. I don't want to think of him with anyone else. I want him to be mine alone, however impossible that may be. So, I change the subject.

"What's it like at Dante's?"

"The mansion is *amazing*, Aurora," she gushes. "You wouldn't believe it. Even the guest rooms have king-sized beds, and the food is wonderful. They have this chef, Marisa, and she's unbelievable, all the Italian dishes she makes. It's just like when Mama used to cook."

I smile. I'm glad that Francesca doesn't seem too traumatized by everything. I know that *I* have nightmares, but I'm glad she seems to be taking it well.

"And the pool?"

"Salt water," she says. "Heated. It's *ridiculous*, Aurora."

I laugh. "Wish I could see it."

"Why don't you? Nico could just bring you here, and you could hide out with me."

I pause, thinking. I don't want to go back to Dante's because I want to stay with Nico, but I can't tell her that.

"Nico says it's dangerous to keep moving around. He says Marco must be on the road."

"Yeah, I guess so," Francesca says, sounding like she's

pouting a little. "Don't worry. Dante's working on catching Marco and he'll be dead in no time."

I blink, a little taken aback. "You want Marco to be killed?"

"Of course I do. Bruno was the one I really loved, you know? He really cared about me. Marco just saw me as a possession." Her voice shakes a little. "I don't know if I'll ever love someone the way I loved Bruno."

"I'm sorry, Francesca," I say softly, and she sniffles.

"It is what it is," she says flippantly, although I'm sure she's grieving more than she lets on. "It's the life we lead, right?"

"Right," I say flatly. I don't always like the life we lead, but she's right. It is what it is.

"Maybe I'll never love again." Francesca pauses. "Or maybe I'll make out with Angelo this weekend."

I snort out a laugh. Nothing really gets Francesca down. "Nice to see that you're still the same old Francesca."

"Better believe it, baby," she teases. "Call me more often, will you? I know you have to be bored out of your mind."

I glance over at Nico who's now lying out on the lawn chair in a pair of trunks. His abs glisten with the sun oil he's put on his body.

"So bored," I say dryly.

We hang up and I walk over to hand the phone back to Nico. He places it on the ground, looking up at me from under the rims of his sunglasses.

"You feel better?" he asks.

I smile. "Much. Francesca seems to be taking things well."

Nico snorts. "Nothing bothers that girl. Everything just rolls right off her back."

"That's a good quality to have," I comment, and Nico shrugs. "I wish I was like that," I say softly, and Nico frowns, reaching up to grab my hand and tug me down into his lap.

I don't realize that I'm trembling until he runs his hands over my arms. It's warm outside, but I have goosebumps.

"Hey," he says softly. "You're one of the strongest women I've ever met."

"I am?" I'm uncertain that's true. I'm shaky right now, just thinking about what I've seen, about the nightmares I keep having.

"Yeah," he agrees, kissing along my shoulder blade. It makes me shiver for completely different reasons. "You went through so much, and you're still standing."

I give him a weak smile. "Thank you, Nico."

"I meant it," he insists, and shifts me around to face him, kissing along the side of my face, little open-mouth kisses.

I lean closer to him, putting my hands on his shoulders as he trails his hands from my hips up to the outsides of my breasts. I'm just wearing my bikini, and he deftly unties the back of my top, letting my breasts bounce free.

Nico hums and darts forward to take a nipple into his mouth, running his tongue around the peak slowly, almost torturously. I moan, rocking my hips forward against him hardening beneath me.

He pulls away, looking into my eyes. "You're beautiful, *principessa*. You know that?"

I don't know that, but I don't dare contradict him, not when he's looking at me with those intense sea-green eyes, not when he moves his hands to my ass, rolling his hips up beneath me. His erection presses against my hot sex and I can feel myself getting slick beneath the fabric of my bikini bottoms.

Nico grunts and shifts sideways, flipping me over onto my back, the lawn chair groaning with the weight of us both.

I wonder for a panicked moment if it's going to break, but it doesn't. It's one of those expensive ones, so I shouldn't have worried.

I untie the bottoms of my bikini myself, impatient, and toss the fabric to the ground. I've gotten a lot of use out of this bikini over the past few week, and I'm grateful for it. It must be magic if it makes Nico want me this much.

Nico doesn't waste time, sliding into me, and the glide is easier because I'm so wet, so ready for him.

"Fuck, *principessa*, were you always this tight?"

I groan loudly, arching my back, clenching my inner muscles around him until he hisses.

Nico leans down and kisses me hard, sliding his tongue into my mouth as if searching it.

He rolls his hips into me, his chest brushing across my nipples, and I moan into his mouth, dragging my nails down his shoulders. I can't seem to help myself, and Nico doesn't seem to mind.

He's got scratches from a couple of nights ago already on his back from me leaving them the last time we were in this position.

"You're such a dirty girl," he grunts. "Always ready for me, aren't you?"

"Yes, Nico," I moan. "Only for you. Only want you."

"That's right," he croons, rolling his hips slower, dragging his dick along my g-spot until I'm breathless. "Only me, *principessa*. Remember that."

How can I forget? Nico's the only man who's ever wanted me like this, ever made me feel this way.

He's looking at me so intently, down into my eyes instead

of my breasts, instead of my body, instead of where we're joined together. "Gorgeous girl," he says. "My strong, beautiful girl."

Pleasure jolts through me when he calls me his, and I'm coming around him in moments, rolling my hips up into his thrusts.

Nico kisses me again, nipping my lower lip, when he comes inside me, and then he breaks away to kiss where he bit me.

"Sorry, *principessa*. You get me all riled up," he mumbles, and I giggle.

"I love that I get you all riled up," I admit.

Nico looks at me, raising an eyebrow and propping himself up on his forearms, his body still pressed against mine, still pulsing inside of me.

"Of course you do," he says. "Look at you." He trails his hands across my breasts, flicking along my nipples until my inner muscles contract around him again weakly. He chuckles and kisses my mouth softly, almost chastely.

"I'm not much to look at," I argue, and I'm not sure why I suddenly feel so self-conscious. I don't mean to fish for compliments but it's like I'm starved to hear them from Nico's lips.

"You're crazy," he mutters. "You're gorgeous, built in all the right ways." He gives me a hard look. "And don't tell me you think you're ugly or something."

I blush, looking away. "I mean, sometimes I do," I admit.

Nico scoffs. "Crazy," he repeats again, putting a hand on my cheek and kissing my nose before he pulls out of me, shifting to pull his trunks back up where he'd shoved them down. He stands up and holds out a hand to help me, and I stand up, naked, my skin warm in the sunlight.

He leads me into the living room and I put my head in

his lap, watching television. Francesca may think that my stay at the safehouse is boring, but wild horses couldn't drag me away.

12

NICO

It's been two weeks since the call with my sister and Aurora is still having a few nightmares, but tonight she had a particularly horrific one. She woke up where we'd both fallen asleep on the couch gasping as if she couldn't get any air inside her lungs.

"*Principessa*?" I call, and she looks at me, her brown eyes desperate. "Breathe, baby," I tell her, hoping that she mirrors me when I breathe in through my nose and out through my mouth. Eventually, she does, her brown eyes searching my face. "It's okay, just breathe."

She does as I say and then throws herself into my arms, burying her head against my shoulder and straddling my lap.

My heart aches for her as I stroke her long hair.

"It's okay," I tell her. "It's all going to be okay."

She finally calms down, stops trembling, and then she sits up, sniffling.

"Sorry," she mumbles, her eyes red from crying.

"No reason for apologies," I assure her. I want to ask

about the nightmare but I don't want to get her started all over again.

"I just haven't been sleeping well," she murmurs, brushing her hair back from her face.

I nod slowly. I would like to say the same, but sleeping next to Aurora I've been sleeping like a baby, which honestly terrifies me.

I've been thinking that I need to put some space between us. I've been thinking that I'm getting a little too attached, a little too domestic, so when Aurora goes to shower, I go out onto the terrace for my unlit cigarette routine. It's been a while since I even needed it.

Dante answers the phone after a couple of rings, sounding annoyed.

"Nico, must you always call me so *early*?"

I chuckle. "Sorry, *capo*. I needed to ask you something."

Dante yawns. "Ask away. I'm up now."

"I thought about what you said. About how I could bring Aurora there, have you take care of her and Francesca."

"Yeah? Is your little sister's best friend driving you nuts?"

"Something like that," I mumble. "What do you think?"

"I think the drop-off might be hairy. Especially given the car chase you experienced a while back. He's surely got another car, and he's looking out for you."

"I'm in a different car now," I argue.

Dante snorts. "You think that will stop him? He's always been good at tracking people down, my father hired him to find a couple of 'missing people' once or twice."

"Shit. You're right, but we might try it anyway. She's getting stir crazy, and so am I."

I don't know if that's really true. I've been pretty content to spend time with Aurora, exploring her body and talking to her about her life, but that's just going to end up getting me in trouble. I've never had real feelings for a woman, and I don't plan on starting now. I don't want anyone close enough to me to hurt me or to be used against me. That's one of the number one wiseguy rules I've set for myself.

"You can give it a try, but I'd hunker down for a week or so," Dante suggests.

"Gotcha. Thanks, *capo*."

I hang up and Aurora is standing behind me, frowning.

"What was that all about? Did they find him?"

I'm not sure if she looks excited or terrified by the prospect, her brows drawn together.

"Not yet," I say quickly, and her face relaxes. "I was just talking to him about taking you to his mansion so that you can stay there with Francesca." I pause when she frowns again. "Then I could join the hunt for Marco, make myself useful."

"You said you'd protect me," she says shakily. "You said *you* would, not Dante."

"He's plenty capable of watching out for you," I argue.

"I didn't say he wasn't, but that wasn't the deal," Aurora says, crossing her arms over her chest.

I chuckle. "Don't be a brat, *principessa*. I want to get rid of Marco as soon as possible."

"So that you can get rid of me?" she asks, tilting her chin up defiantly.

I frown. "I didn't say that," I hedge, even though that was the reason that I'd called Dante in the first place.

"You might as well have," she huffs, and walks back into the house.

"Aurora," I call. "We need to talk about this. You'll be safer there."

"I'm safe here," she insists. "You take care of me, Nico. You've been there since day one."

"I'll still be around, Aurora, but I can do a lot more in terms of finding him than I can here."

To be honest, I haven't even been doing my due diligence and calling around, not since the first night. It's been a while since I reached out to some of the guys I knew in the life to look for Marco. Is that because I don't want this to be over? Because I want her to stay with me?

"It's dangerous," she argues. "It's really dangerous to be out looking for Marco, Nico, and I can't stand the idea of you getting hurt." Her voice breaks and I grab her around the waist, pulling her back into my arms.

She's still stiff but she leans against me, her forehead on my shoulder.

She's right, it is dangerous, but I'm not so much worried about that. I'm worried about Aurora. It's not that I don't trust Dante to take care of her, but he won't watch her like I do. He's got men that do that for him, and I don't know if I trust them to keep an eye on her.

"Just think about it," I murmur, kissing the top of her head.

"I don't want to think about it. The answer's no," she says staunchly.

"We can't stay here forever," I warn. "He'll figure out our safe house sooner or later."

She trembles just slightly. "You said this place was safer than the last one."

"It is, *principessa*, but nowhere will be truly safe while Marco is still alive."

Aurora swallows hard. "Do you think I'd be safer at Dante's?"

I sigh. I'm not sure if I think she'd be safer there, exactly, but she'd be apart from me, and that's what I wanted, right?

"I don't know," I say honestly. "I just thought it might be good for us to have a change of scenery."

"I don't think so," she says fiercely. "I want to stay here, with you."

I nod and she walks back into the living room, flipping on the television.

I plop down on the couch with a groan, thinking that this day has gone absolutely nowhere. I haven't figured out what to do about my blossoming feelings for Aurora, or where to take her that would be safer and away from me.

But Aurora puts on something mindless on television and turns to me, biting her lip, and I can't help but smile back at her.

"Are you mad at me, *principessa*?" I ask.

She shakes her head, smiling a little, and drops down to her knees, crawling toward me. I spread my legs further, my breath catching in my throat.

"Are you being a dirty girl again, Aurora?" I ask in a low murmur, and she nods, still smirking, spreading her hands across my thighs and moving her hands to the waistband of my sweats. She tugs them down, exposing my half-erection to the cool air, and I look down at her, licking my lips.

She leans forward and down, taking me into her mouth and sucking gently at the head before taking me further, gagging slightly when I put my hands in her hair, wrap her locks around my fist.

I bob her head up and down, and she gags again, choking slightly on my dick, and I grunt low in my chest, feeling my balls draw up.

I would never hurt Aurora, but there's a part of me that just loves controlling her, loves making her do all the things I know she likes. She loves to be used like a sex doll.

She sticks out her tongue, working the flat of it along my

underside, and I grunt again when I spill down her throat. She swallows, choking and gagging slightly, which makes my dick pulse in her mouth and elicits a low groan from my throat.

"Goddamn, *principessa*," I murmur before pulling her into my lap, kissing away the tears that have streamed down her face from gagging so much.

Something feels caught in my throat, some series of words that I've never said to a woman not related to me, and I swallow it down. What am I thinking? I'm *not* in love with her. I barely know her and she's my little sister's best friend. She's off-limits and always should have been.

I know that I should push her away but she still looks pale from earlier, and I hold her as she curls up into my lap and starts to watch television.

I'm stuck with Aurora Costa in more ways than one, it seems.

13

—————

AURORA

I'm straightening up and vacuuming inside while Nico cleans out the pool, and I think to myself how domestic we are. Nico usually makes dinner because I'm simply not that good of a cook, but sometimes I bake cookies or cakes. We watch reality television every week, a show that we both like, and we usually fall asleep on the couch those nights. If we don't fall asleep there, we fall asleep after making love, curled into each other.

It's been three weeks since Nico mentioned taking me to Dante's, and about six weeks since we went on the run, and I can't help but wonder what happens after this.

Right now, it's almost like we're a married couple, how we interact with each other, how we live our day to day lives. After we go home, will Nico just leave? Go back to his little apartment and start hooking up with three girls a week? The very idea makes me want to retch. Of course, lots of things make me want to retch these days.

I haven't been feeling well these last few days, the stress of being on the run and all the worrying are taking a toll on me. I can't eat most of the time and I'm even losing weight, which I'm happy about but Nico finds concerning.

He mentioned it the last time we made love when he had his hands on my hips, looking down at where we were joined. He mentioned how I was getting thinner, and I teased him, asked him if he liked me better this way. He just frowned and shook his head. I guess Nico's the kind of guy that likes curves. Lucky me.

Nico's been obsessed with finding Marco lately, on the phone all hours of the night. I know that this situation can't last forever, but god, I wish at least our little bubble would.

I'm in love with him, wholly and irrevocably, and I don't know what to do about it. I'm falling deeper each and every day and I can't help myself.

Nico walks inside, stripping out of his trunks with a grimace. "Full of algae," he says. "I need to get some more of that chlorine. It's time for a supply run, anyway."

I look him up and down as he stands there naked. "I'll join you in the shower," I tell him happily, but Nico shakes his head, chuckling.

"Not now, baby. I'm covered in gross pool gunk. I'll get the supplies, just make me a list."

I pout. "I'm not going with you?"

"Not this time. I'm meeting up with someone who might have some info about Marco, and I don't want him to know you're with me."

I nod slowly, still pouting but realizing that it's important. It's not that I don't want Marco to be found and taken care of. I'm terrified that he'll find us, that he'll kill me, so I want him gone just as much as Nico does. I just know that when he is, all this will be over. Every wonderful day that I have with Nico now will just be a passing memory, and that scares me.

I finish cleaning while he's in the shower, and I'm washing up the dishes when he comes up behind me and kisses the side of my face.

"I'll be back in an hour and a half, tops," he says, and I nod, turning to kiss him. It's quick and almost chaste.

He drives away and I sigh, looking around the small house. I've done all I can do inside, and I'm going to be bored without Nico. I close the sliding door to the terrace and the pool and draw the curtains, planning to nap on the couch, but something keeps me awake.

Maybe it's the thought of going back to the way things were before we went on the run, maybe the fact that I don't feel one hundred percent, but I toss and turn on the couch, unable to drift off.

I finally get up and walk to the linen closet to find a better pillow or maybe a softer blanket, thinking that might be the reason that I can't sleep. I'm standing in the open closet doorway when I hear something.

It isn't much, just a creak, a small sound like someone stepping on the floorboards out on the porch, but I stiffen nonetheless. It could just be Nico coming back, but somehow, I have a bad feeling about it. Then I hear the door open, and just out of instinct, I walk into the closet, slowly shutting the door. I hold my hand on the doorknob, trying not to breathe.

I wait for Nico to call out, to say *"I'm back, principessa,"* but there's nothing, and I know, suddenly, like a bucket of ice water has dumped on my head, that it's Marco.

Or maybe not Marco, but one of his men, someone that is out to kill me.

I can't breathe even if I wanted to. I take in deep, slow breaths through my nostrils so that it's quiet, but I'm shaking all over.

Footsteps sound down the hall, and I freeze except for the trembling, my heart seizing in my chest. I feel cold all over, like there's ice in my veins.

"Where are you, chickadee?" someone calls, and I don't move. I don't even breathe.

I hear a door open and flinch, but it's not this one. It's the bedroom door, kicked open, and I wait with bated breath as the footsteps come closer and closer to me.

I think for a moment that I'm okay, that he's decided that I'm not here, but then the door is yanked open and I stumble out into the hall, screaming, as something pops in my shoulder where I'm holding on to the doorknob.

"There you are," he breathes, and I look up into his eyes. He's wearing a ski mask but he has deep brown eyes, not blue ones like Marco. "Gonna have a little fun with you before I take you out."

I scream again and finally find my feet, attempting to sprint toward the back, to the sliding glass door out onto the terrace, but the man grabs me around the waist, taking my breath.

"Don't leave so soon, chickadee," he mumbles against my ear, his breath hot against my neck. He moves his hand up, his forearm around my throat as if he's about to strangle me, and I do the only thing I can think of.

I bite him, *hard*, drawing blood and tasting iron in my mouth, and he yelps and lets me go. I stumble forward, almost falling before I make it to the sliding doors.

Something *whooshes* fast past me and stings on my cheek but I barely even notice it, I just need to leave. Now.

Just as I yank the door open, hearing the man's footsteps behind me, a gun is pushed onto my face and I scream.

"Shh," Nico hisses, and I collapse, realizing that it's him. Instead of comforting me, though, he all but steps over me and heads into the house. All I hear as I crawl onto the terrace is this *whoosh*ing sound, once and again, and I recognize the sound from the first time I'd heard it – when Marco shot Bruno in the face.

I gasp, finally getting my breath back, and I army-crawl toward the railing of the terrace to drag myself upright, and then someone comes up behind me and grabs me.

I scream.

"It's okay, *principessa*, it's me," Nico says gruffly, putting his arms around me, and I turn and bury my face in his chest, my breath hitching with high-pitched sobs.

I break. I thought I was going to die, that I would never see Nico again.

Nico holds me, murmuring sweet nothings into my ear, telling me over and over that he'll protect me.

"I'll die before I ever let anyone hurt you again, *principessa*," he murmurs, and then I black out.

WHEN I COME TO, Nico's sitting on the edge of the bed, holding my hand. I blink slowly, my throat feeling parched.

I lick my lips. "Can I have some water?"

Instantly, Nico hands me a glass of water with a straw, and I sip greedily, drinking about a fourth of it as he holds it up for me.

"Thank you," I say, and Nico swallows, shaking his head.

"Are you all right?" he asks, and I blink again, looking down at myself. I try to flex the fingers of my left hand but I can't. It's like something's blocking it, and when I try to move my arm, I cry out in pain.

"My shoulder—"

Nico winces. "I think it's dislocated. I'm going to ask you

to be brave for me, *principessa*. Can you do that? Can you be my brave girl?"

I nod, licking my lips again and bracing myself, but nothing could have braced me for the pain when Nico takes my hand firmly in his and yanks, popping my shoulder back into place. I scream and black spots fade in and out behind my eyelids, but I don't pass out.

"Fuck," I curse when I can breathe properly again, and Nico grips my fingers.

"Can you feel this?"

I nod, unable to speak, but the pain is much better. I can flex my fingers again, squeeze his hand.

"It's better," I croak, and Nico's brows are drawn together, his green eyes searching my face.

"We'll see a doctor," he says quickly. "As soon as we can."

I scratch at my face, realizing that there's a bandage on my cheekbone. Everything comes flooding back to me.

The man, the closet, the way that Nico had saved me. I take in a deep breath, trying not to panic all over again.

"I'm okay," I say finally, scratching at the bandage. "I'm alive," I say, as if proving it to myself.

"You're okay," Nico says, but his voice isn't quite steady. "I'm so sorry, *principessa*."

Before I can answer, he lays his head in my lap and I slowly put my fingers into his hair.

"There's nothing to be sorry for, Nico. You saved me."

"I almost wasn't here in time," he says, his words muffled against the blanket he's put over me. "I shouldn't have left you here alone."

"I'm okay," I say softly, stroking his hair. "I'm alive because of you."

Nico's shoulders are shaking, and I'm shocked that he's

having such an emotional reaction. I can't help but wonder if something else happened while he was away.

I comfort him as best as I can, and I can't help feeling like maybe this has affected us both in ways we have yet to fully grasp.

14

NICO

I only let Aurora rest for a few moments after my breakdown, grabbing the two bug-out bags that I've stashed in the pantry in the kitchen.

There's so much we'll have to leave behind, but I don't care.

I walk into the bedroom and Aurora has her eyes closed. The undersides of them look bruised.

"We have to go, *principessa*," I say softly, and she sits up, swinging her legs off the bed. She gets up slowly, favoring her left arm. "Try not to move it," I warn her, and I take our things to the car, planning to come back and carry her to the car. She follows me, though, putting herself in the passenger side with a wince when I open the door for her.

I close it and throw the bags into the trunk and we drive into the city, going to a nearby parking garage that Dante owns and switching cars again. Aurora looks like she's barely keeping conscious as we switch cars, and I'm worried, biting the insides of my cheeks until I can taste iron.

I should have been there. I should have never left, or

should have taken her with me. I got sloppy. Got complacent. And then Marco's man showed up.

I don't know who he was, but after I killed him, I kicked him, twice, breaking a couple of ribs. I wanted to do worse but I needed to take care of Aurora first, get her stabilized and get her out of there.

I look over at her, at the bandage on her cheekbone. At the time I was pretty sure she'd need a couple of stitches, along with a sling for her dislocated shoulder. I'm still almost sure she does need all that. I curse myself inwardly.

"I'm okay," Aurora says as I speed out of the parking garage. "It's okay, Nico."

"It's *not*," I growl. "It's not okay because we were supposed to be *safe*."

"It's no one's fault. They just...they found us," Aurora says, leaning her head back against the seat.

I notice she looks exhausted, and I curse myself again. With as much anger as I have rolling through me, it's hard to not let it out, but I need to focus on getting Aurora safe and get the doctor there.

I call Dante on the way to the next safehouse, one further upstate.

"Ricci," he answers.

"I'm heading to the safehouse on Willow, upstate," I bark. "Marco found us."

"Shit," Dante curses. "What happened?"

"It was one of his men. The guy dislocated her shoulder. Fucking grazed her with a bullet. He won't be hurting anyone else ever again. I fucking made sure of that."

"I'll send a cleaner," he says.

"Forget that. Send a doctor to Willow," I command. I don't usually talk to the *capo* like this, but Dante doesn't seem to be offended. I guess he knows that I'm upset.

"Got it," he says. "Are you sure you don't want to bring her here?"

I glance over at Aurora. "We'll talk about it tomorrow. Just send the doctor." I pause, closing my eyes for the briefest moment before opening them again. "Please."

"He's on the way. He'll meet you there."

I hang up and Aurora doesn't react, her eyes closed, leaning back against the seat and cradling her injured arm.

I wish I could kill him all over again. Slowly. Maybe I should have kept him alive, questioned him about where Marco is, but I just couldn't help myself. He hurt Aurora, almost killed her.

She could have died. That's what keeps swirling through my head. She could have died while I was out getting supplies. I can't think about it for too long or I'll go crazy, it makes me want to throw my fist into a wall or someone's face.

Aurora rests until we arrive at the safehouse and I take our things inside before coming back out to wake her. I won't let her walk herself, this time, scooping her up into my arms and taking her into the house, placing her gently on the couch.

A few moments later, there's a light knocking on the door. Holding my gun in hand, I go to the door and let Jimmy Sawbones in after seeing him through the peephole. I'm still holding my gun in my left hand when he walks in.

He raises an eyebrow, but doesn't say anything. He's probably had many guns stuck in his face before.

"This the patient?" he asks, gesturing toward Aurora, and I nod.

Aurora looks up at him. "It's my shoulder," she says.

"And your cheek," he comments. "Let's get that shoulder stabilized and then we'll see if you need stitches, yeah?"

He takes her left hand in his and she winces, almost imperceptibly, and I have to look away.

"I popped it back in," I say gruffly, and Jimmy looks up at me.

"Did a good job, Nico. Did you go to med school?"

I snort. "Not exactly."

I've just been around plenty of wiseguys who got hurt, including Dante. You pick things up along the way.

Jimmy takes a sling out of his bag and gently places it on Aurora, tucking her arm into it. She makes a small sound in the back of her throat.

"I've got something that you can take for the pain, don't worry," he says, and takes out a pill bottle, shaking two pills into his hand before throwing me the bottle. "Every four hours, whether she asks for it or not, the first couple days," he orders.

I scramble to the kitchen to get Aurora a bottle of water from the fridge and she takes the pills, looking up at me gratefully.

"Does your cheek hurt?" Jimmy asks. "I'll take a look as soon as that kicks in."

"I don't even feel it," Aurora comments.

Jimmy chuckles. "I wouldn't either, with that shoulder of yours," he comments.

She shifts on the couch slightly as he removes the bandage, but she doesn't wince when he runs his fingers along the underside of the wound.

"Just a couple stitches should do it, but you'll have a scar," Jimmy says, and Aurora makes a face as he sets out the materials – a sewing needle and thread, rubbing alcohol to disinfect the wound, bandages.

"It could be worse. At least, you're still beautiful," Jimmy says. "You could always be ugly with a scar."

I snort out a laugh. Jimmy has a certain way with words.

Aurora chuckles, too, and sits still and quiet while Jimmy stitches her up, just a few whimpers of pain here and there and grabbing tight to my hand when I offer it to her.

I hate watching Jimmy stitch her up, hate seeing the angry red wound, so I look away.

After he's done, Jimmy hums in the back of his throat again, as if satisfied.

"She's been sick," I tell him suddenly.

"I'm fine," Aurora says, just the edge of a slur in her voice, and when she looks up at me, her brown eyes are glassy. The drugs are working, which is good, but I want Jimmy to check her out.

Jimmy raises an eyebrow. "Sick how?"

"She's been throwing up a lot," I say. "Stressed out, I guess."

"I'll check her out," he says. "In private."

I frown. "Why in private?"

"Because I'm the doctor. You said you didn't go to med school," Jimmy says dryly.

He helps Aurora up and leads her to the bedroom, and I huff and go outside for my cigarette routine. Man, I really want to light this shit up.

What the hell could he be examining *privately*?

It's so frustrating! I want to know what's wrong, but at the same time, I guess Jimmy knows what he's doing. It takes about half an hour before Jimmy comes out, gathering his things and putting them back into his bag. He walks outside without speaking to me and I follow him, yelling out his name.

He turns.

"What's wrong with her?" I ask.

"Nothing," he says easily. "Just the shoulder and the cheekbone."

"Yeah? She's not sick?"

"She's not sick," Jimmy says, but there's something in his voice I don't like.

"Jimmy, tell me the truth," I say, suddenly panicked.

Jimmy can't tell me if it's something bad, can he? If it's...God forbid, something like...cancer, there's no way he can test for that here.

"I am telling the truth," he says, and gets into his car without another word.

I head back into the house and knock on the open doorjamb. "Aurora?"

"Hmm?" she mumbles, as if she's half asleep, and I sit down on the edge of the bed, taking her right hand in mine.

"What happened? What did he say?"

"It's nothing," she says, looking up at me with wide brown eyes. "I'll take care of it."

"What do you mean, you'll *take care of it*?"

She frowns. "You don't have to do anything, Nico. Don't worry about it."

"Aurora, what the hell are you *talking* about?"

She looks at me for a long moment.

"I'm pregnant," she says finally, and it's like all the oxygen goes out of the room.

15

AURORA

Nico looks at me, shocked, his face paling, and then he just stands up and walks out of the room. He doesn't say a word to me, and I don't follow.

My head is spinning from the drugs and the trauma and the shock of Jimmy telling me that I'm pregnant.

He said there was no way to tell how far along I am without ultrasound equipment, but I haven't been with anyone else for years, and I know the baby I'm carrying is Nico's. He must know it, too, because he hasn't questioned me.

I was happy at first, almost felt giddy.

Jimmy was just looking at me with intense blue eyes.

"Are you okay?" he asked.

"What?" I felt out of it from the drugs, like this might be a dream I was having.

"Do you want to...take care of it? I have my ways," he said mysteriously, and I shook my head, shocked.

"No. No, I want...I want the baby," I said finally.

He nodded. "Then I'll leave these prenatal vitamins.

Take them every day, and do your best to keep things down. I'll leave some nausea medication, too."

"The drugs you gave me...are they bad for the baby?" I asked, worried, and Jimmy shook his head.

"They won't hurt the baby, don't worry."

I thought to myself that I was going to take it easy on them, just in case.

"Prenatal vitamins, one a day," he said, taking a small bottle out of his bag. I wondered how often he dealt with pregnant women that he just had it in his bag. Then he took out another, smaller bottle. "Nausea medication, as needed, but no more than one every six hours," he warned.

I just nodded, still shocked.

"Are...are you sure?" I asked.

"That's why I had you pee in a cup," he said. "To make sure." He took it out of the trash to show me. It said "pregnant" in the window, and I lost my breath for a moment.

"Don't...don't tell Nico, okay?" I asked.

Jimmy smiled. "Absolutely not. Doctor/patient confidentiality," he promised me.

But then Nico had asked me all those questions and the drugs had me loopy and I'd just...told him. I couldn't help myself.

What am I going to do now? What will Nico want me to do? Will he ask me to get rid of it? I told him that he didn't have to do anything, and I mean that.

He doesn't have to have anything to do with me or the baby, I'll take care of it on my own if I have to. I can be a single mother.

Of course, I would prefer that we be together like it's been for the past six weeks. We've been falling in love, haven't we?

I have been, and I wish he has been, too, but I can't be

sure. It's not exactly like we've talked about it, and Nico hasn't ever been a one-woman man. I know about his proclivities with women in the area, and even though it makes me sick to think of him with someone else, I can't assume that he'll be with just me.

And I'm not the type of woman to be able to deal with my man with someone else. I know that a lot of women do, but I just can't imagine it. It would make me feel horrible to know that Nico was seeing someone else, even now when he's not mine.

I can't imagine tolerating it if we were married.

Would Nico marry me?

I don't know. I don't know anything unless I ask him, so I get up and walk to the door, looking out onto the terrace where he's pacing around with a drink in his hand and an unlit cigarette in his mouth. He doesn't even look toward the door.

God, what will I even say to him? I'm sorry? How can I be sorry that I got pregnant? It's not like it's my fault.

I hadn't exactly thought to bring my birth control while we were on the run like this. And it's not like he ever offered to wear a condom.

I stand at the door for a long moment before I slide it open. Nico freezes, his back to me.

"Nico," I call softly, and he still doesn't look at me. "What do you want me to do?"

He's quiet for a long moment, and when he speaks, his voice is hoarse. "I just want you to rest," he says finally, and that's not the answer I wanted at all.

I brace my back against the sliding glass door, looking at him, my arm in a sling, not moving.

"Just go back to bed, Aurora," he commands.

"No," I say defiantly. "We need to talk about this."

Nico sighs, running a hand through his hair before he finally turns to face me. He looks tired, exhausted even.

"I can't talk about this," he says. "Not now. I need to think."

"Nico, I—"

"Please, Aurora," he says quietly, and I can't force him to speak to me, so I slowly walk back inside, tears burning at the backs of my eyes.

I wish that I could shower, but I'd need Nico's help and I can't ask for it, not now. Instead, I walk into the kitchen and get myself a bottle of water, drinking it all down greedily before throwing the empty bottle in the trash.

I sigh heavily and head back to the bedroom, sliding back under the covers. I guess the drugs work well because I finally drift off, and when I wake up, it's because Nico has stumbled into the room. He crawls under the covers fully clothed, still wearing his jeans and T-shirt, and he smells like whiskey.

But he puts his arms around me, slides his hand down to the soft swell of my belly.

"You're really having my baby, *principessa?*" he asks, his voice slightly slurred.

"Yes," I say quietly, not sure what he wants to hear.

He's quiet for so long I worry that he's dropped off to sleep, but then he finally speaks.

"I'll protect you both for as long as I'm alive," he says fiercely, kissing my neck, nipping at my earlobe, and when I turn over, he kisses me hard on the mouth, hungry.

I kiss him back eagerly but he pulls away, shaking his head as if to clear it.

"Not tonight, *principessa.* You're hurt."

"I feel fine," I say, but I know that's probably because of the drugs and he's right.

"Not tonight," he repeats, pressing his forehead against mine.

I feel tears pricking at my eyes again, and this time I let them fall. Nico cups my face, running his thumbs down my cheeks and being careful of the bandage on my cheekbone.

"Everything's going to be all right, *principessa*," he says, and I can't help but believe him. I just wish I knew what "all right" looks like for us.

I manage to drift off to sleep after just a few moments of his quiet, deep breathing.

16

NICO

I wake up with a vicious hangover, the sunlight streaming through the blinds feeling like spears in my eyeballs. My stomach rolls with the whiskey I ingested the night before, and I reach out for Aurora, groaning.

She's not in bed, and I sit up quickly, more pain spearing through my head.

"Aurora?"

She pops her head into the door. "I'm making pancakes," she chirps, and I blink, feeling like my eyelids are sticking together.

"You are? With one arm?" I ask incredulously.

"It is kind of hard," she admits, laughing a little, and I can't believe she's in such good spirits after everything that happened.

She's pregnant. The thought slams into me like a train, and I feel sick all over again, bolting out of bed and barely making it to the bathroom before throwing up in the toilet. I groan and brush my teeth and wash my face before coming out of the bathroom.

I head into the kitchen to see Aurora standing there at the sink, washing up the dishes.

"I'll do that," I mumble. "You should be resting."

"I feel better," she insists, and I sit down at the table because the room is spinning. She laughs at me. "How much did you drink last night?"

"Too much," I manage, and when she puts a bottle of water down on the table, I drink half of it.

"It was a rough night," she says, and I nod, agreeing, before wincing because it hurts my head.

"Rougher than most," I agree. I'm thinking about the baby. Staring at her lower abdomen, all I can think is that there's part of me floating around in Aurora's stomach right now.

She continues to make breakfast, humming and flitting around the kitchen, doing everything one-handed. I know that I should get up and help her but it feels like my head is going to split open if I move too fast.

"I never really had a father," I comment, not sure what I'm saying, and Aurora freezes, turning around from the stove and looking at me. "I don't know how to do this."

"You don't have to do anything," she says, just like she had last night, and I frown.

"What does that mean?"

"It means that I don't mind being a single mother," she says easily, and I huff out a breath.

"I'm going to be its father," I insist. "I'm going to take care of you both."

She snorts. "Did you just call our baby 'it'?"

"We don't know if it's a boy or a girl, and I'm violently hungover," I defend myself.

"Fair enough." She goes back to flipping the pancakes

and makes me a plate of pancakes with tons of syrup and bacon.

I look at it as if it might bite me, feeling acid rise up in my throat.

"I don't know if I can eat," I admit.

"You should try. Soak up some of the whiskey," she suggests.

Just her saying the word "whiskey" makes my stomach roll, but I take the fork and grab a big piece of pancake, shoving it into my mouth.

I do feel a little better once I eat a few bites, and I drink the rest of my water and some of hers.

She eats happily, not seeming to have a care in the world, and I just stare at her, unbelieving.

"Aren't you worried?" I ask her finally.

"Worried about what?"

"The baby," I say incredulously.

"Why would I be worried? I think I'll be a great mom," she says easily.

"It's not that simple."

"Isn't it? I told you, you don't have to do anything."

"Stop saying that," I grumble. "Of course I have to do something. It's my baby."

"Please stop calling our child 'it'," she pleads, and I laugh.

"You don't know if it's a boy or a girl," I say.

"Of course I don't know. I'm not far enough along. The baby's just a peanut."

"My mom says all mothers have a feeling about it. She says she knew I was a boy and Francesca was a girl."

"I have no idea," she admits, looking down at her belly. "I don't have a feeling one way or another."

"Do you think I'll be a good dad?" I ask her quietly. This

question haunts me. I'm not sure I'm ready for any answer she gives me, but I really need to hear her answer.

Aurora looks at me. "I think you'll be a wonderful dad," she says softly, and my heart clenches in my chest.

"My dad was never around," I tell her. "Not even when he was alive. He was always out on a job. I don't want to be like that. I want to be there for my kid."

"If you want to be, you will be," she says, as if it's the simplest thing in the world.

"You're not afraid? I mean, with the life we live?" I ask.

It's something I've always wondered about. Not that I ever wanted to have children, but I know Dante is having one, I know some of my friends want a family.

I don't know how to separate my family life from the wiseguy life, and I don't know how to tell Aurora that.

"You keep me safe," she says. "You'll keep us both safe."

"Of course I will," I say, but I'm not so sure. I haven't done a great job so far. I see that she's removed the bandage from her cheek and the scar is still angry and red. Just an inch upward and it could have taken out her eye. I wish I'd taken the time to pull out that guy's eyeball before I killed him.

I finish half of the pancakes and groan. "I'm going back to bed," I say.

Aurora stands to clear the table and I take her wrist in my hand, stopping her. "You're coming with me," I order.

"Am I?" she asks, smiling.

"Damn straight. You're pregnant and injured and you need to rest."

"Yes, sir," she mumbles, and that goes straight to my dick, making my lower abdomen heat up.

I stand up and she leads me into the bedroom. I plop

down and grab her around the waist, pulling her with me, and she squeaks, protecting her bad shoulder.

"Sorry," I mumble, but she doesn't seem hurt. I kiss along her back. "Do you think it's okay to still fool around?"

"It better be," she says promptly, and I laugh and then sigh heavily.

"I guess better safe than sorry."

"Absolutely not," she says, pouting, trying to crawl into my lap but I block her with a frown.

"I'm not going to touch you until Jimmy says it's okay," I say firmly.

Aurora pouts and sits on her knees, staring at me. "Are you serious?"

"Dead serious." I stare right back at her.

She leans forward to kiss me and I groan.

"You little brat," I mumble. "I say I'm not going to touch you and then you try to kiss me? Tease."

"I'm not being a tease if I'm going to put out," she says, exasperated, and I laugh.

I know that I should be worried. I know that I should be freaking out about being a father, and part of me is. But I walked around all night, drinking too much and wanting to smoke so bad and thinking about what it would be like to have a son or a daughter, and I've come to some kind of understanding.

I don't mind having a child. I just don't know if I want to be with Aurora forever. I don't know if I want to be with any woman forever. But Aurora doesn't expect that from me, does she? She hasn't said so. She hasn't told me that she wants me to get married or anything like that.

Maybe I'm worrying needlessly. Aurora told me that I don't have to do anything, so surely she's not looking for marriage.

Of course, I'm concerned about what it means to be a father, but I feel excited, too. It's like a new chapter in my life, a curveball that I didn't expect.

I've always considered myself good at rolling with the punches. This is just one that I didn't see coming.

"Not until the doctor comes and says it's okay," I say firmly.

Aurora clearly doesn't like it but she curls up into bed next to me, yawning.

It takes me a long time to fall asleep, but she's out in just a moment.

17

AURORA

A week later, I'm tired of the damn sling I'm wearing and I'm tired of Nico not touching me. I feel a lot better since the doctor gave me the nausea pills, and I stopped taking the other drugs the second day. I'm taking my prenatal vitamins every day, and I'm feeling a hundred times better.

I keep telling Nico that, but since Jimmy can't come out and see me until next week, he won't give in. It's driving me crazy, sleeping next to him every night and not being able to be with him. I look at his bare broad back and shoulders, stare at him every night, but there's nothing I can do about it.

I decide to ramp things up a little since Jimmy's tied up with other emergent situations, and so at dusk, I go skinny dipping in the pool out back.

It's a fancy saltwater one, and it feels good on my injured shoulder, anyway. Nico's out on the terrace, fake-smoking as I call it, and the pool is right nearby, so I know he can see me as I shuck off my dress, throwing it on to the lawn chair.

He turns, his unlit cigarette hanging out of his mouth, staring at me with intense sea-green eyes.

"Aurora? What are you doing?" he hisses.

I shrug. "Not like we have neighbors."

I jump into the pool, swimming gently so that I don't hurt my shoulder, doing a few laps before I come out. I start to towel myself off, my legs first, and then my stomach, my hair. I don't bother covering myself up.

Nico frowns at me. "I know what you're trying to do," he says.

"Is it working?" I ask, and he looks down at himself, at the tent in his sweatpants.

"Fuck, yes," he says with a low groan, and I giggle.

"I figured the whole thing has to work since I don't have any lingerie."

Nico chokes, tossing his unlit cigarette out. "If you were wearing a teddy and stockings, it might kill me," he admits.

I pout. "I'll remember that next supply run."

Nico always makes me go with him on supply runs now, and I don't blame him, after what happened.

He walks toward me, and I just know that he's going to kiss me, but instead, he sits down on the lawn chair.

I promptly climb into his lap, rolling my hips, and Nico clamps down onto my hips to stop me, choking out a moan.

"You're too good at lap dances," he says in a low tone.

"I guess in another life, maybe I was a dancer," I tease, sticking my breasts into his face since his hands are effectively stopping my hips from moving.

"Not in this life," he grumbles, and I giggle.

I love how possessive he is.

"I'm fine," I argue. "I've read that it's very healthy to have sex during pregnancy."

"You have? Where?"

"The internet," I say easily.

"Well, then it *must* be true," Nico says sarcastically, but he's distracted looking at my breasts, so I start to move my hips again, bracing myself on his shoulders.

"Please touch me, Nico," I pant, getting more and more aroused.

Nico looks at me for a long moment. "Okay, *principessa*. I'll touch you, but you can't touch me."

I pout. "That doesn't sound like fun."

"It does to me," he says with an evil smirk, and stands up, his hands under my ass to carry me. He takes me to the bedroom and gently lies me down on the bed.

He sits down next to me on the edge of the bed, looking down at me with his bottom lip caught between his teeth.

"Are you ready, *principessa*?" he asks.

I nod eagerly, spreading my thighs, but he doesn't touch me, not yet.

I whine and arch my back.

Nico hums and drags a thumb across one peaked nipple, and then the other. I gasp and he trails his hand between my breasts, down to my stomach, dipping a thumb into my bellybutton.

"Lower," I groan.

He listens, but he doesn't put his hand against my sex like I want him too, instead caressing my thighs, my calves, shifting higher up on the bed to touch me everywhere. He trails his fingers up along my inner thighs and then back up between my breasts, grabbing them, touching all around my nipples without actually brushing across the peak of them.

I'm gasping, barely able to catch my breath at all the sensations. Usually, it's been fast and hard, rough, sudden, but now it's so intimate and sensual that I feel wet pooling between my legs.

"Nico, please," I plead. "Touch me more."

He finally cups my sex, pressing his thumb against my clit and hooking two fingers inside me, and I moan so loudly that it's almost a growl that comes out of my throat.

"Dirty girl, Aurora," he teases, pressing his fingers deeper, pressing tighter against my clit and using his other hand to drag his fingers across my nipples, slowly and torturously.

"Nico, you're being mean," I pout, and he presses even deeper inside me but it's not deep enough. It's not his cock and that's what I want. "I want more," I plead. "Want you to fuck me."

"No, no," he chides, pumping his fingers in and out of me. "None of that until you get the okay from the doctor. And stop moving so much. You're going to hurt your shoulder, and then I'll have to stop."

I freeze, going ragdoll beneath his touch. "No, please," I beg. "Don't stop."

I'm approaching orgasm quickly, and with one last thrust of his fingers inside me, I come around them, clenching hard.

Nico groans and I can see the tent in his sweats, I know he's hard.

"Let me touch you," I tell him. "Let me make you feel good, Nico."

"No," he says firmly. "I'm taking care of you."

"You don't have to- ahh!" I cry out as he shoves his fingers back inside me, vaulting me into another orgasm immediately. Then he moves his fingers to circle around my clit, sliding through my wetness easily. Nico ducks his head to take a nipple into his mouth and then another, deftly using his fingers to make me fall apart all over again.

I come again and again, and by the fifth or sixth time, I'm tired and sore.

"Not again, Nico, please," I beg, the opposite of what I'd been begging him before.

"Think you can give me one more," he pants, and I can see how much this is affecting him. "Want to taste you."

He settles between my thighs, licking up my inner thighs and biting marks there until I'm nearly wailing for him to touch me again. My body feels hot all over, my thighs trembling. I'm desperate for him.

He laps gently at my clit, circling his fingers around my entrance before sliding just one finger inside and pumping it slowly. He drags the flat of his tongue along my swollen sex and I cry out his name, putting my hands in his hair.

"That's it, *principessa*. Ride my face," he commands, and I grind myself against his face, unable to stop myself. I come again, clenching tightly around his fingers and moaning, and Nico slowly removes his fingers, popping them into his mouth to suck them clean.

"Now," I say, looking down at his tented pants. "Now, fuck me," I plead.

Nico smirks and shakes his head, and stands up a bit unsteadily and walks into the bathroom. I can hear him panting and then crying out, and he returns sweaty and smiling sheepishly.

"I wanted to watch," I pout, and Nico chokes out a laugh.

"You *are* a dirty girl, aren't you?" he asks, crawling under the covers with me and I wrap my good arm around his neck to kiss him. He tastes like me and I moan into his mouth.

Nico pulls away with a groan. "None of that, *principessa*. Time for rest."

"I'll miss this when I go home," I say, and Nico's face

changes, going blank. Panic rises in my throat, like I've said something wrong, like he's going to pull away from me for good, but he cracks a smile and I feel relief wash over me.

"I'm just tired," Nico says.

I know he's been up late searching for Marco, talking to Dante and others in the life, so I don't argue, just cuddle against him.

"Took a lot out of me, holding back like that," he jokes, and I chuckle.

"You won't have to hold back when Jimmy tells me everything's fine," I say, and Nico hums in the back of his throat.

"You don't want me to hold back, do you?" he asks in a low, dangerous tone. "You want me to fuck you hard and rough, don't you?"

"Maybe," I say, feeling uncommonly shy when he talks like this and hiding my face in his neck. "But I think you like fucking me hard and rough," I respond.

"Maybe," he answers, and then he buries his face into my neck, breathing me in.

I hold him happily and it's easy for me to drift off when he's in my arms like this.

18

NICO

I know that I have to talk to someone about Aurora and the baby, that it's driving me crazy not to have anyone know about it, not to talk to someone.

It's not really like I can call my sister, and it's not like we've ever talked about this kind of thing, so I call Dante.

"What's wrong?" he answers, and I curse myself.

I haven't really talked to him since Jimmy came around, and I haven't updated him much, either.

"Nothing. Sorry, *capo*," I mumble. "Just wanted to talk to you."

"What's going on?" Dante asks.

I groan and sigh at the same time. "It's a long story."

"It sounds like you're worried sick about something." He pauses. "Does this have something to do with Aurora?"

"You could say that," I say, looking back toward the closed door. Aurora is still sleeping and I'm standing out in the hallway.

"Let's meet up," Dante suggests, and I frown.

"I can't leave Aurora alone."

"I didn't say you'd be leaving her alone. I'll send Alberto, and you can meet me at that shitty diner upstate, what's it called?"

"Marie's," I say, laughing. We'd once had the worst pecan pie there.

"Marie's," he agrees. "They at least have good coffee."

"The coffee is just okay and you know it," I joke, and Dante laughs.

"See you in an hour."

I walk back inside, and Aurora is sitting up on the bed, rubbing at her eyes.

She smiles and tries to grab me and pull me back into bed.

"Sorry, *principessa*. Have to meet up with Dante," I say gently, and Aurora looks up at me.

"Did he find Marco?"

I shake my head. "No, nothing like that. It's just other business," I lie. "But one of his men is going to come here. He doesn't talk much but he'll keep you safe."

Aurora nods. "Guess I should put some clothes on, then," she says with a grin and I frown at her.

"Yeah, you better," I grumble, and throw one of my T-shirts at her. She puts it on with a laugh and slides on a pair of cut-offs.

Alberto arrives in his own car, a little sportscar that he'd gotten as a present from Dante.

He gets out, wearing a pair of sunglasses, and meets me with a smile.

Aurora is inside, making breakfast, which I declined.

I walk him inside. "Watch her well," I warn him. "She'll try to do too much without that sling on."

"I'll be fine," Aurora says, and then turns to smile at Alberto.

He smiles back.

"I'm Aurora," she says, looking at him expectantly, and Alberto's smile fades and he looks over at me.

"Oh, he doesn't talk," I tell her, and then Aurora does something I never would have expected.

She starts to hand sign to him.

Alberto signs back eagerly, clearly excited to meet someone who knows his language, and I can't help the way my stomach rolls.

Alberto is older than us but he's not *old*, and he's a handsome guy. I can't help but be a little jealous.

"Well, I guess you two have plenty to talk about," I grumble, and I note that Aurora doesn't even kiss me goodbye.

I huff and walk out of the house, getting into the car and driving to Marie's with my head full of possibilities of Aurora and Alberto falling in love.

Even if they do, what can I say? You're mine? When I'm planning to go back home and break things off with her, go back to my own life? I can't do that.

I'm still thinking about it when Dante walks into the diner, wearing sunglasses and a suit, walking over and sliding into the booth across from me.

"You look well," he says, and I look at him, at how tired and rumpled he looks.

"You look like shit," I tell him.

He groans. "Mia keeps having Braxton-Hicks and she's been back and forth to the hospital a dozen times this week."

I have no idea what Braxton-Hicks is. Fuck. Is this a pregnancy thing? Do I have to worry about Aurora getting that too? God, there is so much I don't know, apparently, but I'm also not going to ask now. Maybe I can ask Aurora when I get back to the safe house.

"So, what did you want to talk about?" he asks, looking at me curiously.

"Aurora's pregnant," I say flatly, and Dante's eyes widen.

"Shit, I didn't know it would be that heavy," he says quietly.

"What do you mean?"

He shrugs. "I mean, I've already put it together that you're sleeping with her."

"You have?" I gape at him.

"Yeah, I mean, please, Nico. She's exactly your type and you've been stuck with her what, month and a half to two months? Of course you're sleeping with her."

"I hate that you know me so well," I groan.

"But that you've knocked her up surprises me," Dante says, sipping his coffee and wincing. "Yeah, it's not that great."

I crack a smile. "I didn't mean to knock her up," I sigh.

"You didn't use a condom?"

I shrug. "Didn't exactly have time to pick them up on the run from Marco."

"That motherfucker is sneaky," Dante curses.

"Yeah, he is. There's still no leads?"

"Oh, plenty of leads, but none that have panned out."

I order something simple, just a waffle, because I figure they can't fuck that up much. Dante does the same.

We sit there in silence for a moment before Dante speaks.

"You know, it's different now," he says.

"What do you mean?" I ask.

"It's different, now, how fiercely you want to protect them. Your child and your woman."

"She's not my woman," I snap.

Dante raises an eyebrow. "No?"

"No," I say firmly. "After all this is over I'm going home and back to my life. I'll learn how to be a dad, and I'll take care of her financially, but we're not together."

"So, you're just what? Playing house?"

"I guess," I grumble. I don't like this line of questioning. It's making me think too much.

"You sound a lot like me before I gave in to my feelings for Mia," Dante says quietly, and I don't answer him.

I don't know what to say. I remember Dante when he'd first married Mia, and he had been so focused on the life that he hadn't realized he was really in love with her for a long time. That isn't what my situation is.

We eat our waffles, which are mediocre but not terrible.

"I don't have feelings for Aurora," I finally say, but I know that I'm lying to him and myself. I do have feelings for her, even if I'm not quite sure what they are, if I'm not quite sure what that means. I've never had feelings for any woman, or at least not since high school or before. I've always been focused on myself, always been focused on the life, and women are just for fun.

Dante scoffs but doesn't respond otherwise.

"When is the baby due?" he asks, and I choke on my waffle.

"God, I don't know. I never thought to ask."

Dante laughs. "Well, when you find out, let me know. Mia will be over the moon for our little girl to have a playmate."

"Have you named her yet?" I ask, and Dante shakes his head.

"Not yet. We're still deciding between Alessia and Maria."

I wrinkle my nose. "Alessia is much better," he says.

Dante laughs. "I'll tell Mia you said so."

We finish up at the diner and Dante tips the server generously enough that she's full of smiles before we leave.

She's kind of cute, and before, I would have flirted with her, but for some reason, I'm just not feeling up to it. I guess it's because everything has gone so sideways. I'm stressed out about us not being able to find Marco, stressed about the baby, and I've been almost shot too many times the past couple of months. This has nothing to do with Aurora. Not at all.

At the car, I ask Dante what I've been thinking.

"Do you think I'll be a good father?"

Dante glances over at me. "Nico, I've known you most of my life," he says. "And everything you set your mind to do, you do. If you want to be a good father, you will be."

I smile at him. "Thanks, *capo*."

Dante gets into his sportscar and drives away.

I head back to the safehouse, and I'm glad that my boss is also my friend.

19

AURORA

Alberto and I play cards and sign while we're playing.

First, we talk about Marco.

"We're doing everything we can to find him," he signs.

"I know," I sign back.

"He's like a ghost," he comments, and I nod in agreement. It doesn't take long for him to win three hands in a row and I curse out loud.

He grins at me, gesturing to the cards as if to say we should play something else.

I shake my head, and he looks at me for a long moment.

"Do you have brothers and sisters?" he asks, clearly happy to have someone to communicate with.

"None," I answer. *"You?"*

He nods his head.

I smile a little. *"I'm going to have a family, though. A baby,"* I sign.

Alberto's eyes widen and he grins. *"I love babies. I have three brothers and a sister, all younger."*

We sign for a while longer, talking about his family and

talking about my baby, and then Nico comes in the back door.

Alberto stands, looking a little sad, and I stand up to hug him.

"You made me feel very welcome," he signs, and tears burn at the backs of my eyes. It must be so hard to be unable to communicate.

I sign goodbye after hugging him again and he walks out, past Nico who's glaring at me.

"What were you two talking about?" Nico asks.

"Nothing. Everything," I laugh, and then I notice that Nico's still glaring. "Are you...are you jealous? Of Alberto?"

Nico scoffs. "Why would I be? Just because you were clearly flirting with him?"

I roll my eyes, annoyance washing over me. "You're being ridiculous."

"Am I? He's the first guy you've seen since me and you're all over him—"

"Stop it, Nico," I warn, stalking into the living room. It's pretty irritating, especially since Nico and I haven't even talked about what we are to each other, not even after I told him about the baby.

He follows me. "I just think it's interesting how interested you were in Alberto," he starts, and I huff and whirl around.

"Let me ask you something, Nico. Are we exclusively seeing each other?"

"Of course we're exclusively seeing each other," he says, exasperated. "We aren't around anyone else."

"You know that's not what I mean," I say staunchly. "I mean, will that change when we get back home?"

"I don't know what you're talking about," Nico hedges, but he clearly does.

"Are you going to go back to having three skanks in your bed a week once we're back at home?" I blurt out, anger rising in me, and Nico blinks at me.

"You're the one being ridiculous," Nico says.

I shake my head. "I don't think so. You're jealous over Alberto, who was only here to protect me so that you could go out with Dante and do god knows what, and you can't even tell me that we're going to be exclusive when we get out of this."

"I never made you any promises," he accuses, and I stare at him, blinking.

"So you're *not* going to be seeing me exclusively when we get home? This is what? Just all temporary?"

"Don't say it like that, Aurora," Nico says, looking away and rubbing a hand across the back of his neck. "I told you that I'd protect you and the baby."

"Protecting isn't the same as being together, Nico."

"I never said that we'd be together," he says, looking right at me, and tears start to burn at the backs of my eyes.

"Wow," I say, shell-shocked. I didn't know exactly what feelings Nico had for me, but I assumed that he actually had *some* feelings for me. I guess I was wrong. "I guess that makes sense."

"What's that supposed to mean?" Nico asks, taking a step closer to me.

"Nothing," I mumble, backing up toward the bedroom. "You know what? It doesn't matter because this is all temporary, right?"

"Aurora—"

"So, if I *did* want to talk to Alberto, flirt with him, that'd be okay?"

Nico sets his jaw, glaring at me. He doesn't answer.

"That's what I thought," I say, heading into the bedroom

and slamming the door. It's only lunch time, but I plan on going to sleep. I crawl under the covers and I hear Nico curse and stalk around the house.

I lie down for a few minutes but it turns out that I'm too angry to sleep, so I stand up and yank the door open. Nico, predictably, is pouring himself a big glass of whiskey.

I lean against the doorjamb, watching him. "So, do you think you could get me Alberto's number? We could text," I say dryly, and Nico's shoulders stiffen.

"You can get it from Francesca," he barks, and I chuckle but there's no mirth in it.

"All right. Guess I'll call her tomorrow."

Nico turns to look at me, his sea-green eyes intense. "You're not really going to get his number," he says, like it isn't a question.

I shrug. "I think I'm finally realizing what I've been missing out on. You never know what I might do. I'm thinking I should strive to be more like my best friend – more...impulsive."

"You're just trying to piss me off," he growls, stalking toward me, and I don't back away, looking up at him defiantly.

"You want me to be yours, Nico?"

He looks away briefly and then back at me. "I didn't say that."

"But you don't want me to be his? Make up your mind, would you?"

Nico's hand goes around my throat, not gentle but not so hard that I'm afraid. My breath hitches in arousal, in fact.

"You're already mine," he growls, and leans down, sucking a mark onto the base of my throat. I gasp, arching my back, and he picks me up, ramming his hips against mine.

He's already hard and I can't help rolling my hips against his. "Tell me you're mine," he orders.

"Can't do that," I gasp. "You haven't made me yours."

"Oh, we'll see about that," he says, and yanks down my cutoffs and underwear, sliding it off my ankles while still holding me up with one hand on my throat and his body pressing against mine.

He shifts and unbuckles his slacks, letting them fall to the floor, and he's not wearing underwear.

I gasp when he slides up into me, gasp out his name.

"That's right, *principessa*," he commands. "Tell me who's fucking you this good. Not fucking Alberto."

"Nico," I gasp. "Just you, Nico."

He grunts and thrusts into me harder, sliding my ass up against the wall. I choke out another moan, coming around him, and he thrusts into me harder and harder through my orgasm.

His fingers close around my throat, not quite cutting off my air but close, and I come again as he thrusts into me again and again.

"Tell me you're mine," he commands again, and I look up at him, into his eyes.

"I'm yours." I gasp, my head spinning from lust. "I've always been yours, Nico."

Nico cries out my name when he spills inside me and slowly lowers me to the floor.

"Aurora," he says, releasing my throat and kissing along my neck, but I push him away, hard. He stumbles backward and I lean down to grab my shorts, stalking to the guest room and slamming and locking the door.

I'm already curled into bed when he knocks on the door.

"Aurora," he says. And then, several minutes later. "*Principessa.*"

I don't say a word, just bury my head under the pillow and cry myself to sleep.

The next morning, I wake early and walk into the living room. Nico's passed out on the couch with a bottle of whiskey between his legs and an empty glass on the coffee table.

I don't wake him, just going out to the pool and putting my feet in the water, thinking. I know what I have to do now, but I don't want to do it. I don't want to break things off with Nico, but I don't know how else to do this.

I can't just stay with him all this time, loving him, wanting him. Not when he doesn't feel the same way about me.

I have to make a change, even if it's the last thing I want to do.

20

NICO

I wake up again with a violent hangover and hate myself for drinking so much. I hate myself for what I said to Aurora, too, how roughly I made love to her. She doesn't deserve to be treated that way, but it was like I was possessed. I'd felt like I needed to *own* her, like I needed to show everyone how she's mine.

She's carrying my baby, for god's sake, how can she not be mine?

So, there's this part of me that feels like she is, that doesn't want another man touching her, but there's this part of me that wants to go back to my old life. That wants to go back to fucking three women a week, to not knowing any of their names the next week.

That's the life I've always lived. My safe life. A life without risk. Without hurt. And I can't imagine living any other way.

Or, rather, I *couldn't*. Now I can easily imagine living with a beautiful woman who smiles at me, her hair mussed from sex first thing in the morning. That's the problem. Now I know there's another way, but I don't know how to move forward and I don't know how to go back.

I hear someone banging around in the kitchen and can't believe that Aurora is up and making breakfast.

"Do you want sausage or bacon?" she asks, and I think she's been cooking a lot for someone who told me she doesn't know how to very well.

"Neither," I say. "Just toast."

"You can make that yourself," she says flatly, and makes her own plate, sitting down at the dining room table.

"Listen, Aurora," I start, but she doesn't even look at me.

"Jimmy's coming today," she says, and I look at her for a long moment.

"Aurora, I'm sorry," I say softly, and she shrugs.

"It's fine," she says. "Don't worry about it."

She continues eating as if nothing's wrong, and her blasé attitude is beginning to anger me, but I can't say why. Did I expect her to be sobbing all morning? Not really. But I didn't expect this as well.

I open my mouth to apologize again but then Jimmy knocks on the door and I groan, getting up to let him in.

Aurora leads him into the bedroom so that he can do a quick exam on her, and I wait in the living room, bile rising in my throat from the hangover. I eat my toast and that helps a little, and make myself a cup of coffee.

Jimmy nods at me when he leaves, and I'm grateful for his discretion.

"What'd he say about resuming our activities?" I ask, hoping to lighten the mood just a little.

"He says we're all systems go," she says, but there's something oddly flat in her tone.

"Do you...do you even *want* to?" I ask.

"Well, we already did, last night, remember?"

"Who could forget?" I ask, grinning, but she doesn't smile back.

She just walks out to the pool and takes off her clothes, wearing a one-piece that I'd bought for her on our last supply run together.

Aurora jumps into the water and I frown and go back inside, clearing the dishes from breakfast.

What's going on with her? Is she really still mad at me? If she is, why isn't she yelling at me? Why isn't she telling me I'm a selfish sonofabitch?

Aurora comes back inside after a while and I'm sitting on the couch, staring at the television but not really watching anything.

She starts to walk by me but I grab her wrist, stopping her.

"Are you still mad at me?" I ask.

She pauses for a long moment, and I feel a sense of relief, thinking that *now* she'll yell at me.

But she doesn't.

"No, I'm not mad."

"Something's clearly wrong," I say dryly.

She shakes out of my grip. "No, I just had the wrong idea. Things are different than I thought, that's all."

"What's that supposed to mean?" I ask, frowning.

"I thought maybe I meant something to you. Now I know that I don't," she says plainly, and walks into the bathroom.

I walk in behind her as she strips off her one-piece and gets into the shower. I huff out a breath and take my clothes off, getting in with her.

"We're not done with this conversation," I warn.

"Could have fooled me," she says, turning away from me.

"Aurora," I say. *"Principessa."*

"Don't call me that," she barks, turning around, her brown eyes flashing, and there's a spark. Some signs of life.

"Finally," I say, and she glares up at me.

"Finally, what?"

"Finally, you say something," I say, frustrated. "You've been dancing around the subject all morning, and I'd rather just have things out in the open."

"What is there to say?" she asks. "What is there to have out in the open? It's simple. You want me to be yours but you don't want to be mine. You're just territorial. You want to go back to your old life. I'll go back to mine. That's what will happen when we go back home."

"And until then?" I ask, my heart dropping.

"Until then, we're stuck together," she says, and pauses, rinsing out her hair without missing a beat. She looks back up at me when she's finished, her hair long and slick down her back. "Or I could go to Dante's."

"You said it was too dangerous," I say, my heart dropping even further.

She shrugs. "And you said it isn't. Just be careful taking me, and we'll be all right," she says.

"Aurora," I say softly. "That's not what I want."

"Well, it's what *I* want," she says finally. "I want to be back home. If this is all temporary, I'd rather it be over sooner rather than later."

"You don't mean that," I say, staring at her incredulously, but she doesn't answer, just getting out of the shower and grabbing a towel.

I follow her, again, grabbing a towel and slinging it around my waist as I follow her into the guest bedroom.

"You're wrong, you know," I say.

"Wrong about what?" she asks, putting on a nightie that I'd bought her.

I grab her wrist, turn her around. "You mean a lot to me." Her eyes search my face. "You're the mother of my child."

Her face falls and she looks away. "Yeah. That's all I'll be to you, from now on. Just the mother of your child, right?"

"Quit putting words into my mouth," I warn.

"That's what you said," she says stubbornly.

"That's *not* what I said," I argue, annoyed.

"So then, what did you say, Nico?"

My head is spinning from the hangover and the argument and I'm not sure how to respond. She's right, I want to go back to my old life. But thinking about her with someone else, ever going on a date with someone else, ever letting someone else touch her... it makes me crazy.

"What do you want from me, Nico?" she asks softly, tears welling in her eyes.

"I don't..." I pause. "I don't know," I say finally, dropping her hand, and she nods, sniffling, and heads into the living room. I don't follow, sitting down hard on the edge of the bed.

Where do I go from here? Is she really done with me? Is this really the way that things end?

21

———

AURORA

I know that I have to keep my distance from Nico. He doesn't want me. He wants to be part of the baby's life, but he doesn't want to be a part of my life, and I have to learn to deal with that. I have to be a part of his life for the next eighteen years but without him actually being part of my life. He's not willing to change his lifestyle. He's not willing to let himself fall in love. Not that I'm a prize or anything, but I'm worthy of love in my life. I'm worthy a man who will put me first, and that's clearly not Nico.

It hurts like hell, but there's nothing I can do about it. All I can do is keep myself protected, keep my heart safe. Or at least as safe as a broken heart can be. I have to at least keep it from shattering completely. I have to keep a little bit of it, so that I may in time heal and have something to give of myself when the right man comes. Because above all, I have to hope that the right man is out there and will come eventually, since it can't be Nico.

It's a long drive back to Dante's mansion, and after about twenty minutes, Nico gives me a sideways glance. "You're not talking to me now?"

I shrug. "Nothing to say."

"What's that supposed to mean?" he asks, frowning.

"It doesn't mean anything," I huff. I don't want to have this conversation. It's not like anything will change.

"*Principessa*," he starts, and I look away from him, staring out the window. That name hurts more than he'll ever know.

"I just want to get some rest," I say quietly, and Nico sighs but he doesn't say anything more.

I lean my head against the window and close my eyes, but I know that I won't sleep. My heart aches and my stomach is churning, thinking about what will happen when we get back to Dante's. Nico will go back to his womanizing ways and I'll just be sitting at home, pregnant.

This is not how I wanted things to go between us.

I always imagined having children, one boy and one girl, being happy with my husband. But now, I'm pregnant out of wedlock and by a man who doesn't want me.

I do manage to drift off, because the next thing I know, Nico stops at a diner about half way back to Dante's.

"I thought we could get a bite," he says softly, shaking my shoulder.

I blink the sleep out of my eyes, yawning, and get out of the car, walking into the diner ahead of him. Nico follows, seeming sullen. He's sulking, I guess, but I can't bring myself to care. Not after the fight we had. If this break needs to happen, the sooner, the better, and we both need to come to terms with it.

Nico orders a burger and fries and I follow suit, looking down at the table instead of at him.

"Are you going to be mad at me forever?" he asks, trying to catch my gaze.

I won't look at him. "Who says I'm mad?"

Nico scoffs. "You're clearly mad."

"There's nothing to be mad about," I insist. "This has just run its course."

"What do you mean?" Nico tilts his head.

"It's over, right? You don't want to be with me. So, it's done. It was fun while it lasted."

Nico frowns. "I don't know why it has to be over just because—"

"Just because you don't want to commit to me?"

"Listen, Aurora, it's not like I planned this," he says, sounding exasperated.

"I didn't plan it either," I snap. "I'm sure you've done this with lots of women, right? Had a fling and moved on? What makes me any different?"

"You're pregnant with my child," he says firmly. "That makes it a lot different, *principessa*."

"Don't call me that," I mumble.

Nico sighs, running a hand through his dark hair. "It doesn't have to be over just because we're not exclusive," he starts, and I snort.

"I'm not interested in being anyone's second or third choice, Nico. If you're seeing other women, I don't want to be with you."

Nico's quiet for a moment. "What about the baby?"

"You don't have to do anything," I insist. "You can be as involved or uninvolved as you want to be."

"Of course I want to be involved," he barks. "That's my child you're carrying."

I shrug. "Well, that's up to you."

"I have a life to live, you know," Nico says. "It's not like I want to throw everything away just because—"

"Just because you knocked me up?" I accuse, anger rising up in me. The food arrives and I take in a few deep breaths, trying to calm down.

"Don't be like that, Aurora," Nico says, his voice calm. "We'll figure something out."

"You're right. We'll figure out custody when the baby is born," I say. "Until then, you don't have to do anything."

"I want to go to appointments," Nico insists. "I want to be involved in the pregnancy."

"Like I said, that's up to you, Nico." I pick at my fries, still feeling a little nauseous.

We don't talk for the rest of the meal, and when we get back into the car, I pretend to be dozing against the window because I'm fighting tears and I don't want him to see.

"Aurora," Nico says, and he pauses when I don't answer, keeping my eyes tightly closed. "I'm sorry," he says softly.

Tears begin to trail down my face and I keep my eyes closed, wishing that I could doze off and forget everything that's going on for just a few minutes.

When we arrive at Dante's, I rush inside with him trailing behind me.

Francesca meets me at the door and throws her arms around me, and I hug her back tightly, bursting into tears. I missed my friend and I need her so bad right now, even if she doesn't know it.

"I'm so sorry about everything, Aurora," she says. "I know how much you've been through and it's all my fault."

I'm not crying because of what's happened but because of Nico, but of course I can't tell her that. I sniffle and pull away slightly.

"I'm just glad that you're okay," I tell her, and she smiles, tears welling in her eyes, too.

"I'm home, too," Nico drawls. "And alive."

"Good to know," Francesca says easily, glancing at him with a smile before looping her arm through mine and dragging me up to my room. "You need some rest," she says, and I can't deny that I feel exhausted emotionally and physically from the trip and from the past couple of days.

I'm still crying when I climb into bed and Francesca climbs in with me.

"You look like you need some company," she says.

I smile shakily at her. "I do," I say softly. "It's been a long few weeks."

"I missed you terribly," she says. "Mia's so pregnant she can't swim with me."

I laugh, grateful to have my best friend with me. "I missed you too. Nico isn't much of a swimmer."

"He's a bore," she snorts, and I disagree, given the great time we had in bed, but of course she wouldn't want to hear that. Besides, I suppose Nico is keeping it a secret, at least for now.

I feel a pang of guilt. I've always told Francesca everything, and now I'm keeping a huge secret from her. We've always been best friends and so close, but I can't tell her why I'm upset or what's going on.

I close my eyes tightly and Francesca throws an arm around me. "Get some rest," she says quietly, and I don't think I'll be able to sleep at all.

But with the quiet hum of the air conditioning in the mansion and Francesca's presence, I'm able to drift off within a few moments.

22

———

NICO

It's nearing dusk by the time Aurora wakes up and she and Francesca come down for dinner. I want to grab Aurora's arm, pull her aside and talk to her, but what would I even say? It's not like I'm willing to give up everything to be with her.

Am I?

My chest feels tight every time I think of her not being around. Worse still, the idea of us not being exclusive means that she might start seeing someone else, and that makes my stomach roll.

I'm just territorial. It doesn't mean anything. I care about her, sure, we've been through a lot together, but it's not love.

I don't fall in love.

Dante and I have a couple of drinks before dinner and he catches me up on the search for Marco.

"He's underground," he says. "So far underground that even my toughest men don't like to go looking for him."

I know that means he's staying with men who don't care if they live or die.

"And the rest of his family?" I ask.

"They've given up," Dante says. "I've spoken to his brother and he doesn't want this to go any further. He says that Marco's made his bed, and now he's got to lie in it."

I nod. "That's good news. At least we don't have to worry about the whole family tree coming after Aurora."

Dante looks at me curiously. "What's going on with you two?"

"Nothing," I say quickly. "It was just a fling, and now it's over."

"And the baby?" Dante asks.

"I'll be a good father," I say, determined. "I want to be in my child's life, but that doesn't mean I have to be with Aurora."

Before Dante can answer me, the intercom buzzes.

"It's Carlo Costa," the tinny intercom says. "I was hoping you might have an update about my daughter?"

I blink, surprised. I didn't know that Dante had been in contact with Aurora's father, and suddenly I feel slightly nervous. After all, I've heard that Carlo Costa was a force to be reckoned with in his youth, and I've knocked up his daughter.

Dante instantly buzzes the man in and I follow him out into the foyer.

"You ready to meet your kid's grandpa?" Dante asks, a teasing tone in his voice, and I snort out a nervous laugh.

Carlo Costa is an imposing man, broader and more muscular than I am with a layer of fat on his abdomen. His blue eyes pierce through me.

"Good news, Mr. Costa," Dante says. "Nico here has brought Aurora home."

Carlo's eyes change instantly from discerning to bright, and he swallows visibly.

"Where is she?"

Aurora comes out of the kitchen where she's been helping Marisa with dinner, and she sees her father and instantly runs toward him, throwing her arms around him.

Carlo holds her tightly, kissing her temple. "*Carissima,*" he murmurs. "I've been so worried."

Aurora sniffles and pulls away, looking at her father. "It's been so hard," she admits, crying.

"You've been through so much," Carlo says. "Damn Marco Barone and his—"

Aurora cuts him off. "Don't, Papa. It's not important. What's important is that I'm safe."

Carlo sighs. "You're right." He looks over at Dante and me. "You're safe due to these two men." He nods at us. "I'm forever grateful."

I feel a pang of guilt, thinking that he wouldn't be nearly as grateful if he knew that I knocked up his daughter, but I keep my mouth shut.

Aurora and Carlo talk for a bit and keep close to each other before Aurora glances over at me and asks to be excused. She says she's still not feeling well.

"Dinner will be ready in half an hour," she says. "We'll meet back up then."

Carlo reluctantly lets go of her hand and Aurora ascends the stairs. I watch her with a frown.

"Would you like a drink. Mr. Costa?" Dante asks politely, and Carlo waves a hand dismissively.

"Call me Carlo," he says. "And I'd love a drink."

Dante, Carlo, and I go into Dante's office for another drink. My head is spinning slightly already from the expensive scotch I've already consumed, and so I sip mine carefully.

"Nico, is it?" Carlo asks.

I nod. "That's me."

"You've been keeping my *carissima* safe all this time," he says. "I don't know how to repay you."

"There's no need," I say quickly. "Aurora needed my help, and since my sister was the cause of it, I definitely don't need repayment."

Carlo hums. "Francesca is a bit of a hellraiser, but there's no reason that Marco should have gone off like that. He's a loose cannon and he's needed to be dealt with for a long time."

Dante nods, agreeing. "He's always been like this; he's just never gone this far."

"I used to be a bit of a loose cannon myself," Carlo jokes, gulping his scotch. "Until I had Aurora and lost my wife."

I look at him curiously. "What happened to her, if you don't mind me asking?"

He scoffs. "Some businessman in Chicago happened to her when she was on a trip out there. They ran away together. But I have to admit it was at least half my fault."

"How's that?" I ask. I don't know very much about Aurora's home life, and I can't help being curious. I want to know more about her, and I tell myself it's because she's the mother of my child.

Carlo shrugs. "I took her for granted. Ran around on her, didn't care which mistresses I rubbed in her face. I got too caught up in the wiseguy lifestyle, you know?"

I swallow hard. This is beginning to sound really familiar.

"But she left you for another man. Aren't you bitter?"

Carlo looks at me for a long moment. "I'm not bitter that she left me for someone else." He pauses. "I'm bitter that she left *Aurora*. That little girl didn't deserve to lose her mother."

I promise myself in that moment that I will never leave my child like that. No matter what happens between me and

Aurora, I will be part of that child's life. I'll be a real father, and I'll do my best to protect the mother of my child and my child.

I feel a pang of sympathy for Aurora. She lost her mother at a young age, and I can't imagine what that was like. I lost my father at a young age, but my mother and I have been close ever since.

"Dinner's ready," Mia calls, standing at the door heavily pregnant. I look at her, thinking she looks ready to pop at any moment.

"Thank you, baby," Dante tells her, and then stands up, going to the doorway to give her a kiss.

Carlo smiles at the two of them. When Mia walks away, he speaks to Dante.

"Congratulations," he says. "Looks like you've got it all."

"I do," Dante agrees, and sometimes it is hard to reconcile the man Dante used to be with this new family man.

We head down to dinner and it's lambchops and creamed potatoes and I'm all but salivating. We'd only had a few home cooked meals while we were on the run, and most of those I'd prepared.

It would be nice to eat something prepared by Marisa. I love eating at Dante's because I love her cooking.

Aurora's already sitting at the table next to Francesca. I want to sit next to her, but she still seems angry with me, so instead, I sit next to Mia.

"It's delicious," Aurora says to Marisa as she finishes setting the table, and Marisa frowns.

"You've barely touched it," she scolds. "You better eat to get your strength back."

Aurora smiles weakly at her and cuts into her lamb, taking a small bite. Marisa nods, seemingly satisfied, and sits down to eat with us.

It isn't all that common for the help to eat with the family, but Dante's always been anything but common. Marisa is like a surrogate mother to him, and he treats her like family.

I respect that about him. Coming from a household that doesn't have staff or worked at other families' mansions as staff, being from a household that didn't always have what we needed, it's refreshing.

"How are you feeling?" I ask Aurora, a bit worried about her morning sickness which seems to last all day.

"I'm fine," she says shortly, eating some of her potatoes.

I frown but don't press her. Francesca is looking at me like I've grown a second head, and I look away, focusing on shoveling down my food.

Dante and I both praise Marisa's cooking, and she dismisses us with self-deprecating remarks. It's the Italian way.

I'm hoping that I can talk to Aurora after dinner, but she excuses herself early, saying that she needs to bathe and rest. She kisses her father goodbye, who is also eating heartily and praising the food.

Carlo and Dante chat a bit while I stare after Aurora. I'm not fully present at this dinner because I keep thinking about how angry she is. I also keep thinking about what Carlo said, about how he'd taken his wife for granted and lost her.

Is that what I'm doing with Aurora?

I shake my head to clear it. I'm not in love with Aurora and I certainly don't want her to be my wife. We've just been in such close proximity for so long that it feels weird to be separated from her, that's all.

Right?

23

AURORA

I soak in the bath for the longest time, hoping that it will make me feel better. I managed to eat half my plate for dinner, which is progress since I've barely been keeping anything down. I'm not sure if it's the pregnancy or just because I feel so upset.

I miss Nico, miss being around him and sleeping next to him, and I don't know what to do about it. It's not like I can easily forgive him or go back to being in a physical relationship with him.

That won't work, will it? I wish that I could maintain a relationship with him, at least a casual one, but that's not me. I can't handle him seeing other women, and clearly he's not ready to give up that part of his life. I wish he saw me as worthy, but he doesn't so I really have to let go.

I'm just finishing getting dressed for bed when someone knocks softly on my door.

My heart leaps into my throat, hoping that it's Nico, but instead it's a different pair of green eyes at my door: Francesca.

"Hey, you," she says softly. "Haven't seen you since we

took that nap together, just checking on you. Heard your dad was here."

I smile, thinking of my dad and how grateful he was to see me. Sometimes, growing up, I remember feeling invisible in my own home, like he didn't think of me much.

Now, I'm aware that's not the case, and it feels good. I'm beginning to understand that I've never been as invisible as I thought.

"He was worried sick," I admit. "Surprised me."

"We all were," Francesca says. "I knew that Nico would keep you safe, but I figured you were going crazy stuck with him."

I look away and Francesca frowns.

"But you weren't, were you?"

"I don't know what you're talking about," I say, busying myself making my bed and Francesca grabs my wrists.

"What happened between you and my brother?" she demands to know, and I press my lips together in a thin line.

"That's really none of your business," I mumble, and Francesca scoffs.

"We've told each other everything since we were twelve, Aurora, please," she insists. "Did something happen? Did he..." she pauses, her eyes widening. "Did he take advantage of you?"

I stare at her. "What do you mean, take advantage of me? Of course not!"

"I know that you've always had a little crush on him," Francesca mumbles, pacing around my bedroom. "But I never thought it was anything serious. I never thought *he* would—"

"Never thought he would what, Francesca? Notice me?" Anger rises in my blood as I look at her. Perfect Francesca never had any issues being seen, never had any issues finding any number of boyfriends. And I'm all grown up and no longer jealous of that. She's always had everything, and well.... I haven't. But at least I've stayed true to myself.

"That's not what I meant and you know it, Aurora," Francesca argues, but I'm angry now, and I can't stop the words coming out of my mouth.

"You just can't stand the idea that I might have someone, can you?" I accuse. "You can't stand the idea that maybe someone wants me."

"*Nico*? Why would he—" she starts, and I cut her off.

"Get out, Francesca," I say coldly.

"Aurora, please," she pleads. "Let's just talk about this."

I shake my head. "Not right now. I can't talk about this right now, maybe ever." I put my hand on my stomach, rubbing it unconsciously.

Francesca looks down at the gesture and I see the realization in her eyes.

"Oh my god," she whispers. "Don't tell me that he...he knocked you *up*?"

"It wasn't like that, Francesca, he didn't do it on purpose!" I defend him, and Francesca snorts.

"Sure, he tripped and fell into your—"

"Stop it," I cut her off. "Don't be crude."

Francesca throws her hands up in exasperation. "I don't know how else to be, Aurora. I can't believe that my brother took advantage of your crush and got you *pregnant*."

"It takes two to tango, Francesca," I snap. "And I wasn't exactly just lying there like a starfish."

Francesca blanches, looking at me. "You tell me everything, Aurora. You always have. Why wouldn't you tell me this?"

"Because I knew that you would act like this! I knew that you'd hate it," I try to explain, taking in deep breaths and feeling dizzy. I don't want to lose her friendship but I also want to stand up for myself. I want to stand up for Nico.

"Nico is going to break your heart, honey," Francesca says softly. "That's why I don't want you with him."

He already did, I think, but I don't say it, gritting my teeth and fighting back tears.

"That's my problem." I sigh. "Look, I'm sorry I didn't tell you," I say finally, my voice shaking. "But I have a right to be happy, and I want this baby."

Francesca looks at me for a long moment and then stalks out of the door, shutting it behind her. I sigh again. Francesca can be a bit of a brat, but I hope that she comes around. After all, I want her to be the aunt this baby deserves.

I try to calm down, taking deep breaths, and then I follow her out into the hallway. She's not there, but I hear yelling coming from Nico's room and I roll my eyes.

I decide that I need to decompress and I walk down the stairs and out toward the pool. My father is there, in a pair of swimming trunks, his feet in the water. He's had plenty to drink and I can tell by the glassy look in his eyes, but he's not a big drinker so I'm not worried.

I wish I could have a glass of wine myself.

It's been a really long few weeks.

My father smiles at me as I kick off my shoes and sit next to him, putting my feet in the water next to his.

"Glad to have you back, *carissima*," he mumbles, and I lean my head against his shoulder, seeking comfort.

He puts an arm around me, and it feels nice to have this moment with him. We don't have many father/daughter moments. Usually we're in the same house but doing different things. He won't let me in to the things he gets up to, the things he's not supposed to be doing because he has a bad heart. He's still very much in the life despite his ailing health, and I know that.

But it's the way that we make money. The alternative is what, he gets a regular job? Minimum wage because he's never finished school? It's not like he's going to do that, so I try not to complain. But I worry about him.

"How's the ticker?" I ask him quietly.

He thumps his chest. "Still ticking."

I laugh. "I guess that's the best I can hope for."

"How are *you, carissima*?" he asks, and I blink, surprised, but don't lift my head from his shoulder.

"I'm okay, Papa," I say, although that's not really true.

"You have a certain look, *carissima*," he says, and then I do lift my head to look at him.

"What does that mean?"

"You look lovesick," Papa says softly, and tears spring to the backs of my eyes.

It's like for the first time in a long time, he sees me, and it makes me feel comforted and not alone.

"I *am* lovesick," I admit, and Papa nods, looking down at his feet which he's kicking in the water gently.

"Nico, right?" he asks, and I swallow hard.

I don't answer, but Papa seems to know.

"He seems like a good man," he says. "Takes care of you."

I bite my lip. "Yeah," I answer, not sure what else to say. I don't want to tell my father that Nico doesn't want me, that he's gotten me pregnant and he wants to keep seeing other women.

"I always knew you'd fall in love, *carissima*. You've got a big heart, lots of love to give." He looks over at me with a serious gaze. "Just make sure that you give it wisely."

I nod slowly, taking in his words. Maybe I need to back

off even more from Nico. Maybe it's just something that I can't control, and I just need to protect myself.

My father has given me a lot to think about, and a lot of comfort, so we sit there for a long time, my head leaned against his shoulder, his arm around me.

If only life could always be so simple as it is in this moment.

24

NICO

I've just finished talking and drinking with Dante and I'm a little drunk and considering going into Aurora's room when my sister bursts in the door, her eyes wild and angry.

"What the hell do you think you're doing?" she barks.

"Jesus, what's gotten up your ass?" I mumble, and then Francesca puts both hands on my chest and shoves me. I'm not prepared and I'm a little tipsy, so I stumble backwards, sitting down hard on the bed.

"Aurora Costa, that's what," she seethes. "You knocked her *up*?"

Oh shit. I knew that this was coming, but I didn't expect it so soon.

"Fuck."

"Fuck, indeed," Francesca agrees, clearly fuming and pacing around my bedroom. "How dare you take advantage of my best friend like that?"

"Take advantage of her? Francesca, she was a very willing participant—"

"Ew!" Francesca yells, covering her ears like a little kid. I roll my eyes.

"You asked," I shoot back. "And you have no business coming in here and yelling at me—"

"You're going to hurt her," Francesca says, and I sober, guilt rushing through me.

"You don't know that," I say softly.

"You've already hurt her," she says. "I can see it in her eyes when she's around you, Nico, she looks at you like....like—"

"Like what?" I ask, curious.

"Oh, shut up," Francesca grumbles. "I'm not going to out my best friend's deepest thoughts and feelings just because you want to stroke your ego."

I'm genuinely curious as to what Aurora feels, but I keep my mouth shut, knowing that my sister will just get angrier and angrier.

"Look, we're going to have the baby and co-parent," I start, and Francesca scoffs.

"You think that's what she wants? You're an idiot, Nico," she says, raising her voice. "You don't see her."

"What the hell does that even mean?" I ask, exasperated and looking up at her, and Francesca groans.

"See, you're so *stupid*. I can't believe she ever deigned to sleep with you."

"Thanks for the vote of confidence," I drawl, and Francesca glares at me.

"You're going to do right by her," Francesca says, pointing her finger into my chest.

"Who says I'm not? Like I said, I'm going to be there for her and the baby."

"In what capacity?" Francesca demands to know. "In between fucking your strippers and various bar girls?"

I take a deep breath through my nostrils, trying to stay calm. In a way, Francesca is right, and I know it. It's something I've been thinking about ever since we've returned home, but at the same time, it's none of my sister's fucking business.

"I'm going to handle it," I say flatly, and Francesca just stands there, staring at me like I'm the dumbest thing she's ever seen.

"You'd better," she mumbles. "If you don't, I'll kill you myself."

"Good to know," I say, rolling my eyes. Francesca's all bark and no bite. She always has been. I'm her big brother and she's always deferred to me eventually, and she will about this. She just wants to be a brat about it first.

"I'm serious, Nico. That girl has a big heart, and if you break it—"

"I don't know what you're talking about," I say quietly. "She's just as much to blame for this baby as I am, and we agreed to stay casual."

"Sure, she agreed to stay casual," Francesca says sarcastically.

"She did!" I insist, although in reality, I'm not sure she did. It was more like I said I didn't do relationships and even though she was kind of angry about it, Aurora accepted it.

What else am I supposed to do? Give up my whole life? I don't know if I can do that.

"She's not that kind of girl, Nico, and you know it."

"She's never said that," I mumble.

"I know it! She's my best friend, like a sister to me, and you've probably already broken her heart!" Francesca's voice sounds impassioned, angry, and beseeching, as if she wants me to change my mind.

"What do you want me to do, Francesca?" I ask finally, and she sighs.

"I want you to leave her alone," she says quietly. "Let her down easy, but leave her alone."

"I can't do that," I say simply, and it's not because she's pregnant with my baby. It's not because Francesca wants me to. It's because I simply don't want to give her up. I don't want to stop what I'm doing with Aurora because I *like* her. It's not love, of course. It can't be, but it's something, and I think I want to explore it.

"You're such a fucking asshole," Francesca mumbles, and walks right back out the door.

I sigh, thinking that I should follow her, thinking that I should probably go and talk this through, but I'm too tired.

I wait for a few moments, until I can't hear her footsteps down the hallway, and then I leave the room and I walk over to Dante's office, knocking lightly on the door.

"Come in," he calls, and Mia is perched on his lap, looking about to burst and smiling at him. She kisses his cheek when I walk in and nods at me as she walks out the door, seeming to know that we need some time alone.

"Hey," I say tiredly, plopping down in the chair across from his desk.

"You look like shit," Dante says bluntly, and I snort.

"Thanks a lot," I grumble, but I know he's right. I haven't been sleeping well without Aurora in my bed, and I don't like to think about what that means. It's just that I got used to it while we were away, that's all.

"You seem conflicted," he continues, and then he gets up and pours us both a drink.

"You're an angel, Dante."

He laughs. "Maybe a fallen one."

"Any news about Marco?"

Dante tilts his head. "Maybe. I've got a line on a few abandoned warehouses in the worst parts of the city that he might be in. The Rizzos are siding with him."

"Shit," I cursed. The Rizzos might be the most dangerous famiglia in New York state, not just the city. They do horrible things, running scams, sex trafficking.

We all make our money in different (mostly illegal) ways, but they go too far. They always have.

"Fabio is in on it?" I ask, speaking of the head of the famiglia, the *caputo*.

"Unfortunately," Dante responds. "Him and a half dozen others who have been kicked out of other famiglias."

Men who are kicked out of famiglias instead of killed are dangerous men indeed. It means they survived torture, ratted someone out, and somehow managed to get away, so they are out for blood.

I take in a deep breath, blowing it out through my mouth with force.

"Well, we have to go after him," I say firmly, and Dante stares at me like I'm stupid.

"No, we don't," he says. "I'm not putting my men in danger for Marco Barone."

"It's not for Marco," I hiss. "It's for Aurora. It's for my *child*."

"Listen, Nico," he starts. "I know how you feel."

"Like hell you do," I snarl, unable to stop the fear and anger that's rising up inside of me. Dante is a dangerous man to get angry at, but I can't help myself. "It's not your family that's in danger."

"My family's in danger just by having her here," Dante argues, not quite losing his temper but I can tell that it's close by the vein in his neck popping out.

"I'm sorry," I say finally after breathing deeply for a moment to calm down. "It's just... I'm worried."

"Of course you are. I don't blame you. But if we go off half-cocked, not even knowing his actual location..." he trailed off.

"Then people will get killed," I finish, and Dante nods in agreement.

"Good men work for me, Nico, including you. I don't want anyone to get popped."

I sigh. "I can't keep sitting here and doing nothing, Dante. Can you give me the locations? Just to put my mind at ease?"

Dante scoffs. "Do you think I'm stupid? I know the first thing you'll do once you get the information is go after Marco. Just give me a few more days. I'll get a better lead on his location and we'll go in knowing what to expect."

"As much as we can know what to expect," I grumble, but I can't argue with his logic. It won't do me any good to go after Marco and get killed, let my kid grow up without a dad.

"In the meantime, just try to relax," Dante says, and I bark out a bitter laugh.

"Relax," I say. "Sure."

I finish my drink and leave the office before I say something that I'll regret.

As I walk past Aurora's room to get to mine, I trail my fingers along the door, wishing that I could see her face, just for an instant.

It isn't love, I think. *It can't be.*

25

———

AURORA

Francesca and I head out to the pool the next morning as if nothing happened. She doesn't comment on Nico or my pregnancy, just acts like everything's normal. I don't ask what she said to Nico. I'm too embarrassed.

I can't be angry at her for taking up for me, but I hope that she didn't tell Nico anything personal – like how I've had a crush on him basically my whole life.

I feel like I look a little chubby in my bikini, so I wear a one piece with cutouts right above my love handles.

"You look great in that suit," Francesca says, as if she knows I feel insecure.

I smile at her gratefully. I was wrong last night to accuse her of wanting me to be invisible. I know it isn't her fault that she's so beautiful and straight-forward and that guys flock to her.

She's always been lovely to me, and instead of apologizing, I lean against her and she hugs me from the side.

All is forgiven, just like any other time we've ever had a

fight. It's one thing I love about being friends with Francesca. She never holds a grudge.

We do some laps, and when I get out at the shallow end of the pool, walking up the steps, I see Nico standing in the doorway of the indoor pool.

His eyes are on my body, slowly moving up to my face, and I swallow hard.

God, I still want him. Even with everything that's been going on, even after everything he said about not giving up his old life, I still want him. He's taken off his shirt, just wearing a pair of tight swim trunks, and I try not to look at his body.

Francesca glares at him but doesn't speak, just wrapping a towel around herself.

"I'm going to take a shower, Aurora," she says, and winks at me. I know it's her way of giving me and Nico some alone time.

"Hey," Nico says as he approaches me, his voice low and soft. It sends a shiver down my spine and I try not to show it.

"Hey," I answer awkwardly, not sure what to say. "Came for a swim?"

He puts one arm over his chest to stretch it and then the other, and it's impossible not to stare at his muscles bulging.

"A small one," he answers, and then he smirks. "But I think I'll stay longer for the view."

I feel my cheeks heat up.

"Can I come and visit you tonight?" he asks. "In your room?"

His green eyes are searching my face, and I lick my lips.

"You still want a physical relationship?"

He shrugs. "I don't like the word relationship, but sure."

I want to scoff but I'm honestly too turned on, looking at

his muscular body, listening to the low tone of his voice in my ear.

"You can come to my room," I say softly. "Anytime."

He grins. "Good to know."

But then I ruin it, because I just keep talking. "It's not like anyone else will want me, anyway, not now."

Nico frowns. "What are you talking about, *principessa*?"

My cheeks redden further and my chest constricts at the pet name, and I look down at my feet.

"I mean, I'm all fat and pregnant now. No one will look at me like that."

"*Principessa*," he says, trying to catch my gaze but I won't look at him. Finally, he cups my chin in his hand, forcing me to look at him. "You're crazy," he says softly, almost a whisper. "Any man would be lucky to lay eyes on you."

My breath hitches in my chest. "You think so?"

"I know so," he says.

"So, if I meet someone else while I'm pregnant..." I don't know why I say it. I guess I'm trying to make him jealous, but it doesn't work because he just looks away.

"You're a free woman," he murmurs, and then he walks past me and leaps into the deep end of the pool, swimming quickly, his back muscles rippling.

I look away and sigh, putting my hands to my red cheeks, and I wonder if he'll visit me tonight. Do I want him to? Do I want to put myself through this all over again?

I glance over at him again, at his body and his handsome face as he comes out of the water at the shallow end, and it feels like there's something boiling in my lower abdomen.

Yes. I'll put myself through anything just to be with him, in whatever capacity I can.

I'll take what I can get.

I MEET Francesca in the dining room with a plate in front of her and sit down next to her.

"You need to eat something," Francesca says, but my stomach feels funny after talking to Nico.

"Francesca," I say seriously. "I need to talk to you."

She looks up at me from her plate of fruit and slides it to me. "Okay, but you should eat."

I take a piece of honeydew and eat it slowly, and it does make my stomach feel better.

"This thing with Nico," I start, and she waves her hand dismissively.

"I'm not upset with you or anything, babes," she says easily. "I just don't want you to get hurt."

"That's the thing, though," I argue quietly. "I want to be able to make my own mistakes. I know that I'm not very experienced and that you are, but you make *lots* of mistakes."

Francesca scoffs. "Tell me about it."

I continue without looking at her. "So, I need to know that you're not going to interfere. Not with Nico, not with this baby."

"That baby is my niece or nephew," she argues. "I'm going to interfere plenty."

"Okay, fair enough," I laugh, glancing up at her and she's looking at me with a little smile.

"You're gonna be such a good mama," she says, and tears spring to my eyes.

"I'm glad you think so," I say softly, sniffling and trying not to cry.

"I know so," she insists. "You're such a kind and loving

person, Aurora. That's why I'm worried about you and Nico. He doesn't feel things the way that you do."

"I think maybe he does," I say softly. "He just keeps it buried deep inside."

"Maybe," Francesca agrees. "But you can't fix him, Aurora. You can't lose yourself trying to have him."

"I won't," I say, more confidently than I feel. That's really the essential problem with me and Nico, isn't it?

I want him so badly that I'm willing to give up a part of myself. That's what I've been doing, all this time. But yet, I've just agreed to have him in my bed later tonight. Knowing that I want more. Knowing that he doesn't.

I sigh when Francesca keeps looking at me. "I understand what you mean," I assure her. "And I'm going to try really hard to keep being myself, okay?"

"That's all I needed to hear," she says, and then Mia comes into the living room with a big plate of leftover pasta. She smiles at us.

"Mind if I join you ladies?" she asks.

I nod and so does Francesca.

"Of course, it's your house," Francesca says.

Mia laughs. "I like to be a good host. Feel free to share this pasta with me. I'm eating for two, not four."

I snort and take my fork and eat a little off her plate, my eyes widening. "This is delicious. Marisa made this?"

Mia smiles. "Dante, actually," she says.

"Wow, this is better than anything Nico has ever cooked," I say, even though he's cooked some great meals for me, this one is phenomenal.

Francesca laughs, always happy at any dig to her brother. They're so close, but at the same time, they butt heads so often.

"You're eating for two, also, I heard?" Mia asks me softly, and I flush.

"Yeah," I agree.

"I've been trying to get her to eat!" Francesca says.

Mia hums in sympathy. "It's so hard to eat the first couple of months," she says. "I was nauseous for the first five months. They say it's four, but it was five for me."

I groan. "Don't tell me that."

I have to admit that it's nice, to be able to talk about it, not have it be some secret. It's nice to have someone like Mia who's going through it to talk to.

"And then I had the weirdest food aversions," Mia continued. "I love onions and garlic, but the first few months? I would throw up if I so much as smelled them."

"That sounds terrible," Francesca says, her eyes wide.

"No onions and garlic as an Italian should be considered torture," I say, and Mia laughs.

"It gets better." She pats her big stomach. "It gets easier." She winces and I look at her.

"Are you okay?"

"I'm okay. She's just kicking away in there. You want to feel?" She takes my hand and places it on her stomach, and I feel a little bump. Then another.

"Wow," I breathe, my eyes feeling watery again. It seems like I'm crying all the time. "That's beautiful, Mia."

"You won't think so when yours is sleeping with his butt in your ribs," she laughs, and I smile, wiping at my eyes. She leans in closer to me. "The crying gets better, too."

I feel encouraged and eat more pasta and fruit, my stomach feeling more and more stable. I chat with Mia and Francesca late into the evening before dinner, and finally, we realize that the guys are missing.

"Where did Nico and Dante get off to?" Francesca asks, and Mia shrugs.

"They're probably drinking in the office," she says. "I'll take them a plate later."

I look at her curiously, wondering what it is they'd be talking about. Not that I'm worried Nico would talk about me, why would I be? He doesn't care that much.

Mia and I complain about not being able to have wine with dinner and Francesca announces that she's *never* getting pregnant and we talk through dinner, Marisa joining us.

It's kind of nice just having women at the table, and we barely miss the guys' presence.

26

———

NICO

After my swim, I go to shower and spend some time in my room, making calls. Angelo is my first call, since he's nearby.

"Nico, what's up?" he answers, sounding out of breath.

"Are you busy?" I ask him, and he scoffs.

"There's been nothing going on for weeks," he complains. "I'm bored out of my mind."

"Good to hear," I mumble, "because I've got something really exciting coming up."

"Oh, do tell," he says brightly.

Angelo is a bit of a loose cannon, but everyone knows he gets the job done.

"Marco Barone," I say, and I can practically hear the grin in Angelo's voice when he answers.

"Oh, hell yeah."

"He's hiding out underground," I tell him. "Abandoned warehouses in the slums, that kind of shit."

"Sounds like a good time. When are we moving out?"

"Soon," I tell him. "I'll call you once I get the location."

"Perfect. I just got a new piece and I've been dying to use it."

I laugh and hang up the phone. It's good to know that I have people on my side, especially Angelo. He's always up for anything.

I walk to Dante's office and knock on the open door.

He looks up from his phone.

"I'm sorry about yesterday, *capo*," I say sheepishly.

Dante waves a hand. "It's okay."

I come inside and shut the door behind me, sitting heavily down in the chair.

"Tell me more about Marco Barone," I say firmly, and Dante's lips thin.

"I don't know, Nico. I don't want you going off half-cocked..."

"I won't," I insist. "I've called Angelo and he's down to help."

Dante raises an eyebrow. "Angelo? Isn't that a little risky?"

"Not if I'm there," I say. Dante knows that I'm responsible and won't take unnecessary risks the way that Angelo probably will.

"He's a good man to have in your corner, but he's hard to control," Dante says. "That's why I only hire him when everything else fails."

Angelo is one of those guys who has a lot of street cred and full Sicilian heritage, but doesn't want to be head of his *famiglia* and only wants to work freelance for Dante. He's a lone wolf, and a dangerous one at that.

"But he is in my corner," I argue. Angelo has been a good friend to ours. He's probably my best friend other than Dante.

Dante sighs. "All right, Nico. I'll give you the location but you have to promise me that you'll be prepared."

"Only if you promise not to tell Francesca and Aurora," I say, and Dante nods in agreement.

"The girls shouldn't know what we get up to."

"That's the wiseguy way," I say with a smirk and Dante laughs, nodding in agreement.

I finish my drink. "Another?"

Dante pours us both another. "Why not day drink?" he asks with a chuckle.

"It wouldn't be the first time," I point out.

"God, you remember that bar? Where was it?"

"On fifth. In the worst part of town," I laugh, remembering.

"We spent all night there, until it was daylight."

"Took home a few girls, from what I remember."

"Four, I think. Then we just passed out before we could do anything with them," Dante chuckled.

I laugh with him, enjoying spending time with my friend. I'd missed it while we were out running from Marco.

"Enough reminiscing," Dante says suddenly. "I'm not that guy anymore."

"Was it hard?" I ask him, curious. "Giving up that life?"

Dante gave me a half-smile. "No. It was the easiest decision I ever made."

"Really?"

He snorted. "No, not really. It was hard. It's hard to change, Nico. But it was worth it. I did it for Mia and for our little girl."

"When's she due?" I ask.

"Soon," he says. "Any day. I worry myself sick thinking about Mia going through labor."

I swallow hard. I hadn't thought about that, not yet. It's

like the baby is just some possibility, some future problem. I hadn't thought about all the pain that Aurora will have to go through. I think about the scar on her face, how angry that scar makes me.

Not because it makes her less beautiful. Because Marco Barone had been the cause of it. Been the cause of her pain and trauma.

I hate him, and I want to take him out. That's why I need Angelo, and that's why I need Dante to give me the location. At least he's finally agreed to it.

"I don't know if I can do it," I admit.

"Do what? Go after Marco?" Dante asks.

I shake my head. "That, I can do. I mean about changing. About being a different man for Aurora."

"You can do that, too, if you want to," Dante encourages. "It's not easy, but it's possible. I'm living proof."

"You make it look so easy," I grumble.

Dante chuckles. "Well, you saw me before. When I was conflicted, just like you. It's easy now because this is the way it was supposed to be."

"You really think that? You believe in soulmates?"

"I got shot saving Mia, and then she came back into my life and she's going to give me a beautiful baby girl. How could we not be soulmates?"

I think about it, how I feel when I see Aurora, how it's different from Dante and Mia. Aurora was always in my life, for a long time. She's been Francesca's best friend since they were kids. But the way it all happened, Marco shooting Bruno, her seeing it, me being the only one who could protect her – Is it fate? Is that what soulmates are?

I shake my head to clear it, sucking down my second drink and pouring myself another. I don't think I can have this conversation sober.

"I don't have to change if I don't want to," I argue stubbornly. "I can still be a good father if I'm not with Aurora."

"You can," Dante agrees. "But do you want to?"

I tilt my head. "What do you mean?"

"I saw Mia so much differently when she got pregnant," Dante says. "I saw her as mine, you know?"

Jesus. I do know. I see Aurora as mine, and I have even before she got pregnant, but I don't say that. Not to Dante.

"I don't know if I feel that way."

Dante clears his throat. "So, you'll be fine when she finds someone else?"

I freeze, my blood running cold. "What do you mean?"

"Pretty young thing like Aurora, she won't stay single long," he drawls, and my skin heats up with anger.

"Don't talk about her like that," I snap.

"Interesting," Dante mumbles.

"Oh, fuck you," I grumble, and shoot down my third drink. "I wouldn't care if she found someone else," I lie. I *know* I'm lying. I *know* that I would go crazy if another man so much as touched Aurora.

"You don't mind anyone else touching her? Kissing her? Making—"

"Don't," I say, holding out my hand to stop him.

Dante laughs. "You're in trouble, Nico, and not because you're going after Barone."

"Shut up," I grumble, and Dante laughs again, and I hate him.

I hate him because he's right, and now all I can think about is some possible future in which Aurora has my baby and has another man at her side. God, what if she gets married to someone else? What am I supposed to do? Stand there at the wedding with our child and grit my teeth and bear it?

Why do I even feel this way? I've always been a little territorial, but nothing like this. Is this what Dante's talking about with Mia? Is it fate? Soulmates?

I've never believed in any of that. I can't start believing it now.

Can I?

27

AURORA

I'm full and tired by the time dinner is over, and I go to lie down for a few minutes. It's still early, but I fall asleep nevertheless.

I wake up late at night. Looking at my phone I notice that it's two in the morning. Someone is banging on the door and I squint at the doorway.

"Come in," I call, and Nico all but falls into the room, stumbling toward the bed.

"Are you going to see anyone else?" he asks, his words slurred, and I just stare at him, sitting up in bed with the duvet still over my body.

"What the hell are you talking about?" I ask. "You're drunk."

"So?" he asks, walking over and climbing onto the bed clumsily, plopping down beside me on top of the duvet.

"So, you don't know what you're saying," I say, looking over at him and fighting a laugh. His dark hair is falling into his face, his shirt half unbuttoned, showing bronze flesh in between. He smells like whiskey. "Have you been drinking all day?"

"I am stressed," he says. "You're having my baby and you're going to be seeing someone else."

"I don't have anyone in mind," I tease, but then my tone goes serious. "But I do have that right. We're not together."

"You do *not* have that right," he mumbles, turning toward me, burying his face in my stomach where I'm sitting.

"No?" I ask, my fingers immediately falling to play in his hair. I can't help myself. I feel like it's been too long since he's last touched me, and he's cuddling my legs like he can't bear to let me go.

"No," he says firmly, pulling the covers down and I laugh and throw them off onto the bed when he fumbles. He covers my body with his own, looking down into my eyes.

"You're mine, Aurora," he says softly.

"Am I?" I breathe, wishing he would say that he cares for me, even a little. Even if it's not enough, it'd be something.

"Yes," he says firmly, but he doesn't say anything more. He doesn't say what I want him to say, but he kisses me, and that's almost enough.

His tongue delves into my mouth and I meet it with my own, kissing him deeply, my eyes tightly closed.

Nico sits up on his knees, reaching under my nightie to slide his fingers under my panties.

He just brushes against my clit and I moan loudly.

"Look at me," he murmurs. "Look at me when I'm making you come."

My eyes pop open and his are dark green with desire as he presses two fingers inside of me, checking me. I'm already slick for him, but he takes his time opening me up, hooking his fingers upward.

I gasp, arching my back. He's the only one who has ever

made me feel this way and I want to tell him, want to ask him if he feels the same, but I've lost my breath.

Nico rolls his hips against me with his fingers inside me and I can feel him hard and heavy against my pelvis.

But he keeps pumping his fingers in and out, keeps making me gasp until I spasm all around him, coming, crying out his name.

"That's right, *principessa*. Come for me," he croons, and I think I'm done but then he keeps moving his fingers, keeps hooking them upward to drag across that spot inside of me that makes my eyes roll back in my head. He brushes his thumb against my clit and I come again, black spots appearing behind my eyelids.

"Wow," I gasp. "Nico, that was—"

"It's not over," he murmurs, stopping me with a long kiss that makes my skin heat up even more than it already was.

He slides down my body, kissing my nipples through the fabric of my dress, my belly button, my hipbone. I gasp in breaths, having trouble keeping enough oxygen through all the sensations.

Nico kisses my clit softly, slowly sticking out his tongue and dragging the flat of it against me and I spasm, kicking.

He takes my ankles in his hands, slides them across his shoulder blades so that he can press his mouth closer against me, latch around my clit.

"Oh, my god," I gasp.

"Not god," he says sharply. "Say my name, *principessa*."

"Nico," I manage, trying to breathe. "Nico, please..."

I trail off, still having some dignity, enough to be slightly embarrassed that I'm begging him.

"Please what, *principessa*?"

"Please make me come again," I whisper, and he doesn't

waste any time, suckling on my clit and pumping his fingers still inside me.

I shudder all over when I come a third time, and then he removes his fingers, getting up on his knees and fumbling with his pants before shoving them down and freeing himself.

I'm so blissed out I can barely move but it turns out that I don't have to. Nico flips me over onto my stomach, spreading my thighs with one of his.

"Ready, *principessa*?" he asks, and I'm not sure I am. I don't know if I can come again without exploding, but Nico doesn't seem to care.

He slides inside of me, slow, inch by inch, and I cry out, my moans muffled into the pillow.

Nico tugs on my hair enough to make me squeak, and licks across my neck. My squeak turns into a moan.

"Want to hear you, *principessa*. Don't ever be quiet with me."

I choke out a moan as he starts to roll his hips, torturously slowly. My fourth orgasm builds inside me slowly as he thrusts into me.

"God, oh god, *Nico*," I cry out, almost a scream, as I come around his cock and Nico groans loudly.

"*Principessa*," he moans. "Aurora."

Then he pumps into me a few more times, his thrusts unsteady, and I feel him spill hot inside me.

I'm gasping for air against the pillow now that he's dropped my head, and Nico kisses along my spine.

"Sorry, *principessa*," he mumbles. "Wanted to make you mine. Wanted to remind you that you're mine. Both of you."

I blink, surprised, and roll over onto my side. Immediately, Nico slides up against me, putting his arms around me tightly.

"That baby in your belly makes you mine," he says, just an edge of a slur to his voice.

"Yeah?" I ask, and he nods, burying his face against my neck. "You want me to be yours?"

"No," he mutters, and I can tell he's on the edge of falling asleep. My heart drops. "You're already mine."

His hand trails down to cup my pouch of a stomach, and my heart flips around in my chest instead of dropping to my toes.

"What does that mean?" I ask, but he's already asleep, snoring lightly against my ear. I bite my lip. How am I going to do this?

Can I really carry on just a casual relationship with Nico when he acts like this? When he calls me his but then he doesn't really mean it? Or if he does, I'm his but he can't be mine.

I don't know if I can go on like this. I thought I could. I missed him so much I thought some Nico was better than none. But I don't know if my heart can handle it. I'm almost sure I'll be destroyed if I let myself have just the scraps of him he is willing to give me.

It takes a long time for me to fall asleep.

When I wake, Nico is gone, and all I have is the memory of what he said and our lovemaking etched into my mind.

Did he mean anything that he said? He was drunk but was he *that* drunk?

I don't know how to feel. All I know is that I want Nico so badly that I want it to be true. Maybe my hopes are coloring what he really means.

I need him a hundred percent sober when he tells me that he wants me.

28

NICO

I 'm hungover as hell when I wake up in Aurora's bed, and I barely remember the night before. I know that I should stay in bed with her, wait until she wakes up, but I can't remember what I said to her.

I know it must have been something stupid, because of the way I was feeling when I left Dante's office.

My head was spinning and I felt like I needed to see her, needed her viscerally, the way you need food or water to survive. I know that I said something that might hurt her later, when I tell her that I didn't mean it.

They say *in vino veritas*, which means in wine, there's truth, but is that true? Did I mean whatever I said to her last night?

Can I face her now?

My plan is to play dumb, pretend like nothing ever happened.

"When are we going back home?" Francesca asks when I walk down to the kitchen. "I'm worried about Mama."

"I hired someone to help around the house and I've been calling her," I defend, but I know that isn't enough. Our mother won't tell us when she's not well, and then she'll just injure herself trying to cook and clean around the house even with help. I know that we need to check on her, but I can't even think about leaving Dante's.

I'm worried that the second I do, something will happen to Aurora. And no matter how I feel at the moment, I can't imagine something happening to her and the baby. It would kill me.

I'm starting to remember bits and pieces of last night, of cupping Aurora's face and looking into her eyes, seeing the scar on her cheekbone and seething.

I need to know she is safe. I have this deep need to protect her and the baby, especially now, and to make sure nothing happens to her, I'm going to go after Marco Barone.

Today.

I stalk into Dante's office as soon as I see him awake.

"You look like you're on a mission," Dante says, looking down at his phone.

My burner phone dings and I look down at it. He's sent me a few addresses.

"That's the best I've got," he says. "And as you see, they're all in the underground. I can't promise you how many men he's got now that he's gotten in with Fabio Rizzo."

"I know," I tell him. "Thank you."

Dante sighs and reaches around his neck to hand me the key he always wears, ever since his father died.

"This is the key to the armory. Take what you need." He groans, "Angelo, too, although tell him not to steal them."

I grin. "No promises there."

"I know," Dante grumbles. "But still."

"I appreciate this, Dante," I say.

"I'd go with you if Mia wasn't so close to giving birth—" he starts, and I cut him off.

"I know that, *capo*. You stay here with your girls. And watch over mine."

"Aurora, too?" Dante asks with a raised eyebrow, and I take in a deep breath.

"Aurora, too."

For better or for worse, I know that my feelings for her are stronger than just *like*. I don't know what love is, but after last night, after a night of imagining her with someone else and then making love to her, making her mine, I know that whatever love is, I might be feeling it.

And I'll tell her that. As soon as I take out Marco Barone.

"I'll watch over them," Dante says, not pressing me, and I'm grateful.

I call Angelo on my way downstairs.

"You ready to go?"

"With bells on," Angelo drawls.

"I'll pick you up," I tell him, and then hang up the phone.

Then I hear a voice call out, "Nico? Where are you going?"

I turn around to see Aurora standing halfway up the staircase.

"*Principessa*," I murmur, my eyes fixed on the scar on her cheek. She seems to notice, putting her hand up to her face, and I catch her pretty eyes instead.

"What's the rush?" she asks, yawning. "It's early."

I swallow hard, wondering if I should tell her or not.

"I'm going after Marco Barone," I say finally, not wanting to lie to her, and her hand goes to her mouth now.

"You can't do that," she says quickly, descending the stairs with her hand trailing along the railing. "You're not doing that."

"Somebody has to," I say, heading to the armory. It's in

the back of the house, hidden, but Aurora follows me nonetheless.

"Nico, we need to talk about this," she insists. "I'm safe here. Dante's keeping me safe."

"You won't have to be kept safe if I take him out," I say simply, taking out some hardware from the armory. I pick out a nice little automatic for Angelo, knowing he'll never give it back.

I throw everything into a duffel bag and Aurora's just looking at me, her eyes wide and shining.

"You *can't*," she sobs, following me to the door, and I turn around to look at her, putting a hand on her arm.

"It's gonna be okay, Aurora," I tell her. "Don't worry, *principessa*. I've got this. I've got you."

She hitches in a breath and watches me go, and my heart aches that I didn't kiss her goodbye but I don't think I'd be able to leave if I had.

I swing by and pick up Angelo and he whistles when I open the duffel bag and show him the contents.

"I'm keeping that automatic," he says, and I snort out a laugh.

"I figured."

"You don't even have to *pay* me for this," Angelo continues, hopping in the car as I shut the trunk. "I've been wanting to get rid of Marco Barone ever since he hit on my girlfriend."

I raise an eyebrow as I get in the car. "You don't have a girlfriend."

"Not anymore," he says mysteriously, and I don't ask questions because Angelo wouldn't tell me anyway. He keeps his personal life to himself, and I don't blame him. In this lifestyle, it's better to keep your mouth shut.

We travel to the worst parts of the city, checking out the

closest warehouse first. I'm pretty sure it's not the one because it seems like a ghost town, and sure enough, there's nothing but rats and mold in there.

"How many of these are there?" Angelo complains.

"Just three," I answer.

"Three?" he whines, always impatient, and I chuckle.

"Listen, if we don't find him, you can shoot the rats," I joke.

"Promise?"

I laugh, loud and open, and I feel like I've been missing this part of my life ever since I went on the run with Aurora. I'm the muscle, just a low-level thug, and it's something that I like about my job. I don't have to worry about a reputation or money or the hierarchy of wiseguys. I just get to beat and shoot, and it's something that takes my mind off the shit going on in my life..

Maybe it's weird, but I do love my job.

Angelo, on the other hand, is a different breed entirely. He lives and thrives off adrenaline and he's as blue-blooded as Dante.

We hit the jackpot on the second warehouse, and we know it as soon as we pull up. There's an Escalade parked on the corner of the street, too close to be anyone but Marco or one of his guys. No sane New Yorker would park such a nice car in this area.

"He's got to be in there," Angelo says, and I nod, parking in a sketchy parking garage and taking out the duffel bag. I pack a semi-automatic into my spine sheath and then bring the bag full of ammo and bigger weapons with me.

"Don't shoot him," I tell Angelo. "I want to do this bare-handed."

"Love a bare-fisted fight," he agrees. "Leave me some."

"You can have everyone else, for all I care," I tell him. "Marco is mine."

I can't wait to throw my fist into his face, feel the flesh give beneath my fists. I think about the scar on Aurora's face, the nightmares that she had. I think about my baby in her belly and how he wants to off her, and my blood boils with rage.

But outwardly, I'm calm. Cool as a cucumber. It's why I'm suited for this job.

"What's your beef with him, anyway? You were never close to Bruno."

"It's about a girl," I say, cocking the gun as I pull it. We're approaching the warehouse and I don't want to be caught unprepared.

Angelo's eyes widen, but he doesn't have time to ask more questions because a popping sound comes from the other side of the warehouse.

Angelo hefts the automatic in his hands and a yell and a thud let me know he's hit his mark without me ever laying eyes on the man. Angelo is a sharp-shooter and that's why I need him in my corner.

I'm better with my hands, but he's a better shot, and we'll make a good team.

Another guy comes around the corner, stupidly yelling and giving away his position, and it's clear that the men with Marco are ex-wiseguys, or haven't been wiseguys at all. And from the look of them, they're too far into the drug life to ever climb out.

The one I shoot in the chest is skinny with barely any teeth, and he goes down easily with just the one shot.

Angelo and I have silencers, but since these men don't, Marco will be on the move.

It takes me a moment to identify him because there's a

scattering of men like cockroaches when we kick down the warehouse door, but the glint of his gold watch tips me off. Marco's sprinting like he's running track, climbing out the back window of the warehouse, but I make it over there and grab his foot, pulling him back in.

He draws his gun but I punch him right in the nose and his aim goes wild, shooting up into the ceiling. Marco looks the worse for wear, having lost weight, looking dirty, and I wonder if he's taken up drugs as well. Francesca wouldn't like the look of him now.

Bullets are sounding all over the warehouse, but I ignore them.

I black out as I beat him, feeling his facial bones crunch under my knuckles, and when I fall over, I'm not sure why.

Angelo runs over to me, his face pale.

"Shit, Nico. You're hit," he says, and I look down. I don't see any bullet hole, but my back feels like it's on fire all of a sudden and something is trickling down my spine.

I look up at Angelo and then I black out.

29

AURORA

As soon as Nico leaves, I run upstairs to Francesca's room, banging wildly on the door.

She comes to the door with her hair mussed and her eyes squinted since she hasn't put in her contacts yet, glaring at me.

"It's seven in the goddamn morning, Aurora," she complains, but then she sees the look on my face and stills. "What happened?"

"Nico just left," I babble. "He went after Marco."

Her green eyes widen. "Oh no, he fucking didn't," she curses, walking past me and running almost right into Dante. "How could you let him leave?"

Dante shrugs. "I'm not his keeper."

"Don't give me that," she hisses. "You know going after Marco right now is suicide—"

"Don't claim to tell me what I know, Francesca Andretti," Dante says in a low voice, channeling his *caputo* attitude, and I swallow hard.

I don't want Francesca to get into trouble.

"We're just worried," I explain, and Dante's face softens.

"I know, but you both know that Nico does what he wants. I couldn't have stopped him if I wanted to."

I know that's true, but at the same time, I can't help being a little angry at Dante for giving him the information about Marco.

Francesca sees the look on my face and turns to me, putting an arm around me.

"Listen, Aurora. Nico's an idiot for going off like this but he's also really good," she tries to assure me. "You've seen him in action. He's going to be okay."

"You don't know that," I whisper. "You don't know that he's going to be okay, and I'm here, pregnant with his baby!" My voice raises into an almost shout.

Mia comes out of the bedroom, looking tired but concerned. She takes one look at me and Francesca and puts together what's going on.

She takes my arm. "Come with me," she says. "Let's talk."

I can hear Francesca still arguing with Dante and think how bold she is to argue with a man who's as powerful as he is and also has protected us all this time, but I can't worry about my best friend right now.

All I can do is worry about the father of my child.

"Every time Dante goes out on a job, I worry that he's going to never come home," Mia says quietly, leading me to her bedroom and sitting me down on the bed.

I'm nearly hyperventilating and she keeps rubbing my back and I think that's the only thing that keeps me from falling apart.

"I haven't told him," I whisper. "I haven't told him how much I—" my voice breaks and tears start to roll down my face.

"You love him," Mia says, and it isn't a question.

I hitch in a breath. "Is it that obvious?"

She smiles. "It is to me. I've been there."

"But Dante's crazy about you," I argue, trying to think of anything else but how Nico might die not knowing how much I adore him.

Mia snorts. "He is *now*. But for the longest time, he was just using me," she admits.

My eyes widen. "What do you mean?"

She waves a hand. "It's a long story, but I'll just put it this way: I fell first, and *hard*. I was seventeen years old the first time I met Dante, and I was lost."

I swallow hard, understanding. "I feel the same way about Nico, but I was probably even younger," I chuckle.

"They're tough guys," Mia explains. "Wiseguys. It takes them time to figure out what love means, how it's different than hatred and death. They experience that all the time, and it's hard for them to change."

"Nico won't change," I mourn. "But it doesn't matter. I don't care about any of that, I just want him to be safe."

"He's going to be okay," Mia says.

"How can you know that?" I ask.

"I don't," she admits. "But we just have to hope."

I have so much hope that it hurts me. I hope that Nico comes home alive. I hope that Nico is a part of this baby's life the way he says he will be. I hope that Nico tells me, one day, that he loves me.

"Hope hurts," I sob, covering my face with my hands, and Mia hugs me to her.

"I know it does, honey," she says, and I bury my face in her shoulder and start to cry.

Nico doesn't return for hours and hours, and all I do is curl up in Mia and Dante's bed and cry. Francesca comes to check on me a few times, trying to be reassuring, but I can see the worry on her face. She's just as upset as I am.

Finally, the intercom buzzes through Mia and Dante's room and I scramble out of bed, rushing down the stairs.

There's a man standing there, one that I don't recognize, with wild eyes, covered in blood. His arms and shirt are soaked with it.

"Call Jimmy Sawbones," he croaks, and Dante puts an arm on his shoulder.

"Angelo? Where are you hit?" he asks.

Angelo swallows. "I'm not," he says. "It's Nico."

That's when I black out and hit the floor hard.

I COME to with Mia holding these awful smelling salts beneath my nose.

"Nico," I gasp, sitting up, and Mia struggles to her feet. She's too pregnant to move quickly, but she does the best she can helping me up.

"Go slow," she warns, but her face is pale and I know something is wrong. I'm trying to remember what it is but passing out has made me so dizzy and fuzzy...

Nico.

I rush into the living room and Nico's on the couch, absolutely covered in blood. Dante and Angelo both have their hands on his back, holding pressure, and Jimmy Sawbones, the doctor to all the famiglia in the area, has just come in the door, rushing to the living room.

I just stare at him, knowing that I'll get in the way if I go over there.

"Did you see the wound?" I ask Mia, and she slowly nods.

"It's bad, isn't it?" I whisper.

"It's bad," she agrees, and I feel faint again but I manage to keep consciousness, tears streaming down my face.

"I can't fix this," Jimmy says almost immediately. "We have to take him to the hospital."

Dante doesn't argue, grabbing his keys.

"Let's go."

"What is it?" I ask Jimmy, clutching at his arm in desperation. "Where's he hit?"

"In the back," he says, not mincing words. "It's stuck in there, and it could be close to his heart."

"Oh my god," I sob, and Mia grabs me as I try to get to Nico.

Francesca's also downstairs, standing next to the couch which now has Nico's blood all over it. Her face is pale and she looks like she's about to pass out.

I go to her, grabbing her and hugging her tightly, and she slowly, very slowly, hugs me back.

"He's going to be okay," I say, but my voice is choked with tears and I don't know if I believe it.

"He's going to be okay," she repeats in a near-slurred voice. She's in shock, and I've been there. I'm probably right there with her because I can't imagine Nico not making it. I can't imagine any scenario where he's not in this world.

"I'll drive you both to the hospital," Mia says quickly as Jimmy and Angelo and Dante move Nico to the car, Jimmy still holding pressure on the wound.

I follow Mia, trying not to look at Nico, trying not to look at the blood soaking his white shirt red.

I feel like I'm standing outside my body, as if I'm on the outside looking in, and its disconcerting.

At the hospital, the police ask a million questions but all of us just keep saying we don't know, that he was in a bad part of town and he must have gotten caught in the crossfire. They don't seem to believe us but none of us care.

They can't charge us for bringing in an injured man.

I keep thinking of all the blood, of Nico's face, how pale he was, almost gray.

I keep rubbing my stomach, waiting and waiting.

Francesca comes to me after speaking with the doctors.

"It's an artery around his heart," she says in a shaky voice. She's holding together so much better than I thought. "He's lost a lot of blood. They're taking him to surgery to remove the bullet now."

"God," I whisper, and I hug her tightly. She's shaking all over.

"I have to call Mama," she murmurs, and I let her go and she walks outside of the hospital.

Mia takes my hand. "You need to sit down. You fainted just a little while ago."

I listen to her, letting her take me to a chair.

I haven't completely broken down yet, not since I fainted, and now I'm feeling it approach like a freight train.

"God, Mia, what am I going to do?" I ask, searching her face, tears bursting from my eyes.

She looks at me and she doesn't have an answer.

I break, burying my face in my hands, and Mia just keeps rubbing my back, not knowing what else to do.

30

NICO

I dream of Aurora. I dream of her with her eyes puffy from sleep, with her nightie bunched up, how she writhes beneath me. I dream of her in that little bikini she wore at the safe house, looking up at me with wide brown eyes.

I remember hitting Marco, beating him so thoroughly that his face was unrecognizable. I remember Angelo's pale, drawn face as I looked up at him. I don't remember being hurt. I don't know where I am when I open my eyes, looking up at the ceiling.

"Nico?" someone says, some sweet voice that I know deep in my heart, and I look over to see Aurora staring at me with wide brown eyes. "Oh my god, he's waking up," she chokes, and I reach out for her and there's a stab of pain in my chest that makes my breath hitch in my throat.

"*Principessa*," I choke out, but my mouth is so dry that I can't make more words. I clear my throat, and as if reading my mind, Aurora brings me a glass of water with a straw.

I sip it gratefully. "What happened?" I croak.

"You were shot," she says, and then she bursts into tears.

I want to take her into my arms but I can't move and it's torture to just watch her with her face in her hands.

"*Principessa*," I manage. "Look at me. Look into my eyes."

She does, her brown eyes wet with tears as they stream down her face.

"I'm okay," I say, although I'm not completely sure I am. "I'm alive."

"It's been two days," she gasps out between sobs. "You had to have open-heart surgery and you've been on a ventilator for two days. You started breathing on your own, so they took it out but then you wouldn't wake up."

I blink, surprised at everything that had gone down. "I'm awake now," I tell her. "I'm okay, Aurora."

"You're not okay," she sobs. "Your poor chest. Your poor heart."

"It's going to be okay," I say with a smile. "You'll take care of it."

She sniffles. "What are you talking about?"

"I love you," I burst out. I can't hold it in any longer, not after what's just happened. "I'm yours, Aurora. My heart and soul."

Her brown eyes widen. "You...you don't mean that. You're just coming to, it's the drugs—"

"It's not the drugs," I say, although they might be loosening my tongue, they're not doing much for my pain. My chest feels like it's been cracked open, and I guess it has.

"Just...save your strength, Nico. I'll go get the doctor."

She starts to get up and I grab her hand, wincing at the pain it causes me. She sits, staring at me, wide-eyed.

"I'm sorry," I tell her. "I'm sorry for everything."

"You have nothing to be sorry for," she insists.

"I have plenty to be sorry for," I say firmly. "I didn't want to change. I didn't want to give up my playboy lifestyle, the wiseguy lifestyle, but when I found Marco Barone, I couldn't stop."

Aurora shushes me. "Don't talk about that here," she whispers.

I swallow, trying to clear my throat. It feels like something's stuck in it, and I don't know if it's from the surgery or just from emotion.

I feel so much, now, when I've been pushing it down inside me my whole life. I feel so much that it hurts.

"I didn't realize how much it was hurting you," I say. "Not until Dante made me realize."

"Dante?" she asks, as if she's too curious for her own good, and I smile.

"Dante asked me what I would feel if you were with someone else," I tell her. "I told him I wouldn't care."

Her face falls and I squeeze her hand.

"But that's just it, don't you see? I would care *too much*, Aurora. I lied to him. I lied to him because I couldn't face my own feelings for you. I couldn't face that things were changing within me."

"You don't have to say all this, Nico," she warns.

"I want to," I say. "I need to. I need to tell you that the only reason that I didn't kiss you before I left to find Marco is because I thought If I did, I'd never leave you. I never want to leave you, Aurora. Not ever."

"Nico, please," she whispers. "I can't have hope right now. I'm just happy that you're alive. You don't have to say all of this."

I clutch at her hand, feeling myself lose consciousness. My vision keeps blurring.

The doctor comes in and I'm irritated, moving around.

"Mr. Andretti, you have to stay still," the doctor pleads. "You have tubes in your chest and they can't be moved."

"He's in pain," Aurora says, seeing something on my face.

"No," I say. "I don't want any drugs."

Aurora's face is pleading with me. "Please, Nico. I don't want you to hurt yourself."

I sigh heavily and then groan because it hurts in my chest so much.

"All right," I croak, and the nurse puts a button in my hand.

"Press this button," she says, and when I do, something warm and relieving washes through me and my whole body relaxes. I feel myself drifting away.

"Aurora," I say, my words slurred. "Tell me that you know I love you."

"Sure," she says, but I know that she doesn't believe me.

I struggle to say more but I can't, I'm fading.

"Nico," she says quietly. "I—"

But then I'm gone.***

When I wake, Aurora isn't in the room with me but I can still hear someone sobbing. When I turn my face, it's Francesca, her face buried in the bed sheets.

"Francesca?" I call, and she lifts her head, sniffling.

"You're so *stupid*," she says, and I can't help but smile, fighting back a laugh because I know it will hurt. Everything hurts.

"Mama says I'm smart and handsome," I joke, and Francesca doesn't smile.

"I'm going to hit you *so hard* when you get out of here," she says, and I look over at her and I don't know if it's the drugs or the fact that I almost died, but I feel so fond of her that I can barely stand it.

"I love you, Francesca," I say, and Francesca bursts into tears all over again.

"Don't say that now, you jerk. You've never said it before."

"I'll blame the drugs later," I say with a smile, and she grabs my hand so tightly that it almost hurts.

Dante comes in after Francesca gets herself together and leaves, and he sighs heavily.

"What about the cops?" I ask, and he shakes his head.

"Don't worry about it. I didn't tell them anything."

"And Angelo?" I ask.

"Not a scratch on him."

"Lucky sonofabitch," I grumble, and Dante laughs and it's a little shaky.

"We're all glad you're okay, Nico."

"Where's Aurora?" I ask.

"Mia made her go home. She says it's too much stress for the baby and she needs to rest."

I nod slowly but I'm a little disappointed. I want to see her.

"Have you changed your mind now?" Dante asks, tilting his head curiously. "About Aurora, I mean?"

"I didn't change it," I say. "I just decided to actually tell myself the truth now. She's my soulmate, Dante. Just like Mia is yours."

Dante smiles. "I always knew it, you idiot."

I snort and then groan because it hurts so much. "Fuck me, did I get shot twice?"

"Only once, but it was bad. We almost lost you," Dante says.

"I'm too stubborn to die," I argue, and he laughs.

"When Aurora comes back—" I start, and Dante cuts me off.

"I'll tell her to come right in," he says, and I smile gratefully. "Now get some rest."

"I'll be fine," I mumble.

"That's an order," he says firmly, and I smile, throwing my forearm over my eyes. Dante leaves the room and I'm left alone and all I can think is that I can't wait to see Aurora, see her pretty brown eyes, even that scar on her cheekbone.

She's everything. Her and my baby inside her, and I can't believe I didn't realize it until now. Now all I can hope is that I can make it up to her because Francesca and Dante are right.

I *am* an idiot.

31

———

AURORA

Francesca and I both are ordered to go home and we sleep in the same bed in my guest room, cuddled up together. We've been through a lot and we need that best friend comfort.

When I wake, I immediately sit straight up in bed, thinking about Nico.

"I have to get back to the hospital," I mumble, and Francesca yawns, grabbing my shoulder so I can't get up.

"Not yet," she says. "You need to eat something. Have to feed that nephew of mine."

I chuckle in spite of everything. "You think it's a boy?"

"Just a hunch," she says.

"I guess we'll see," I say, rubbing a hand over my belly. "But shouldn't we check on Nico?"

"Mama's up there with him now," she says. "You don't have to worry, she'll call me if he sneezes."

I laugh a little. "All right. I guess I'll eat."

My stomach feels like there's a void in it, so I guess it's a good idea.

We walk downstairs and Marisa has made a spread that's unbelievable.

Mia is shoveling food in her face and she looks up at us and smiles.

"Please sit. Marisa cooks for an army and I'm taking full advantage."

Francesca laughs and I manage a smile.

We sit down and eat.

"This is so hard," I comment. "I hate not being at the hospital."

"You need to rest," Mia says. "Get your strength back. You'll be no good to Nico if you pass out again."

After a few moments of all of us eating quietly, Francesca looks at me, tilting her head.

"Have you told my brother that you're in love with him?" she asks, and I choke on my orange juice.

"Who says I'm in love with your brother?" I ask dumbly.

Francesca snorts and Mia laughs at us both.

"Let's be real," Francesca says. "You've been in love with him since you were seventeen. I know it, you know it, but if you haven't told Nico, he doesn't know it. He's stupid."

I look at her, biting my lip nervously. "He said some things at the hospital, but I'm sure it was just the drugs."

"What did he say?" Mia asks, and we both look at her. She shrugs. "What can I say? Now that I'm old and pregnant and married, I look for drama where I can find it."

"He said that he loves me," I mumble, hardly able to believe it even though I was right there when he said it.

Francesca gasps. "Really? He actually said it? It's about time."

"What do you mean, it's about time?" I ask.

"I've seen Nico with a lot of women," she says, and my

nose wrinkles involuntarily. "I mean, a *lot* of women," she continues.

"You don't have to rub it in," I say dryly.

"But I've never seen him look at a woman the way he looks at you," she finishes, and I swallow hard.

"Are you sure?"

"I'm positive," she says. "Nico's an idiot, but if he says he loves you, he means it."

I don't believe it. Not even with what Francesca says. Not even when Nico said it to my face. He was just out of surgery. He didn't know what he was saying.

"And if he told you, you should tell him," Mia points out.

"He knows," I mumble.

"I keep telling you, my brother is stupid," Francesca says, and Mia laughs.

"All wiseguys are when it comes to love," she agrees.

"So, I really have to say it to him?" I ask.

"I think it's time to go to the hospital," Mia says, struggling up with Marisa's help. "Can you drive? I can barely reach the steering wheel."

On our way to the hospital, Mia and Francesca talk idly about this and that, and I'm looking out the window, thinking about Nico.

Surely, he knows how I feel about him. I've been obvious, haven't I?

And what if I tell him and he doesn't remember anything about yesterday? God, that will be mortifying.

I'm still thinking about it when we arrive at the hospital.

I make my way into Nico's room, still lost in my own thoughts, and he's sitting up on the bed, some color in his cheeks.

I smile, unable to help it. He has a slight beard on his jaw, and it looks good on him.

"You look really good for a man who has been shot in the heart," I say, and Nico grins.

"Thanks, I guess?" He looks at me. "Did you get some rest? Eat something?"

"I did," I say, patting my stomach. "It's like I have a food baby and a regular baby."

"When do you go to your first ultrasound?" he asks.

I blink. He said he wanted to be involved and be there, but I didn't actually think he meant it.

"I scheduled it for this week, but since you're in the hospital—"

"Francesca can go with you," he insists. "You need to be checked out. Things were stressful when you got pregnant."

I stare at him, still confused. "Are you on drugs?"

Nico chuckles lightly so he doesn't hurt his chest. "I mean, yes, but that's not what this is about." He frowns. "Is it not okay to be worried about my baby?"

"Of course it is," I say quickly, biting my lip.

"What's with that face?" he asks.

"What face? This is just my face," I insist.

"No, it's not. It's your worried face. I'm okay," he insists. "The doctor says I have to stay here for a few days, but I can go home soon and you can take care of me there."

"I can take care of you?" I ask, shocked.

"Who else is going to do it? Francesca?" He snorts. "She'll kill me on purpose."

I laugh, but I'm reeling. "You want me to take care of you?"

He frowns. "Didn't I just say that? Why, you don't want to?"

"Of course I want to," I say. "But...would it be weird, me being at your apartment?"

"Why would it be weird?"

I open my mouth and then close it again, not sure how to answer that.

I think about Francesca and Mia, what they'd said, about how Nico looked at me, about how I should tell him.

I'm not sure that I can, but… "Listen, Nico, I need to tell you something," I say slowly, and he just looks at me expectantly, so I blurt it all out. "I've kind of had a thing for you since I was a kid, and when we started seeing each other…I really fell in love with you. I fell hard. And I know that I said I was okay with us being casual but I'm just…I'm not, Nico. I need more. I need you."

"Of course," he says easily, and my mouth drops open. "What?"

"Of course. You have me, *principessa*. All of me." He taps his chest gently. "Bum ticker and all."

"What are you saying, Nico?" I ask, hope rising in my throat, but I'm not sure if he's saying what I think he's saying. It's hard to believe, after everything.

"I'm saying what I said yesterday, *principessa*. Don't you remember? I love you. You're mine and I'm yours."

"You… you remember that?" I ask, tears welling in my eyes.

"Of course I remember it," he says, sounding exasperated. "It's the first time I've ever told a woman that I loved her."

"I'm the first?" I ask with a big grin, wishing I could throw my arms around him but not wanting to hurt him.

"The first and only," he assures me, smiling back. "So, you're moving in, yeah? You're taking care of me, and then I'll take care of you until the baby comes, and then we'll take care of each other."

I can't believe it. This is everything I've ever wanted to hear, but I feel nervous, unsure.

"Will we... will we get married?" I ask, not even daring to hope that much.

Nico groans. "I mean, I *guess.*"

I can't help but laugh at his tone. "What does that mean?"

"It means, baby steps, *principessa*. I want you, and I want you forever, but marriage is hard for me to wrap my head around."

I nod slowly, thinking about it.

"So, will you be with me anyway?" Nico asks. "Will you be mine, *principessa*?"

His words echo in my ears. I never thought that I would hear this coming out of his mouth, and here it is.

I just look at him and he looks back, expectantly.

32

NICO

"If you really want to get married..." I start, but Aurora cuts me off.

"I don't care about that," she says. "I just need to know that this isn't drugs, so tell me all of this again when you're off them," she says.

I sigh shallowly so that I don't hurt myself. "It'll be a while before I'm off all of them."

"I can wait," she says stubbornly.

So, we wait. We wait until I'm out of the hospital and then she goes to her first ultrasound and tears well in my eyes when I see pictures of the little peanut.

Aurora moves in with the help of Dante and Francesca and sets up my bed in the living room so that I don't have to go upstairs. We're sitting in the doctor's office at her five month appointment. She's been living with me and taking care of me all this time, even though I'm getting better now.

"Can I tell you now that I love you?" I ask her, and she shakes her head.

"You're still taking pills," she argues.

I groan. "Aurora, this is getting ridiculous. You live here. You take care of me every day. We're together."

"It doesn't mean that you love me," she insists. "It doesn't mean that you really want me."

"How could I not want you?" I asked, frustrated as we sit in the doctor's office. "How could anyone? Didn't I almost die for you?"

She swallows visibly but then the doctor calls her inside.

I rub my hand along her belly while she waits up on the table, feeling my child kick, and it's the best feeling in the world. The baby has been kicking for a couple of weeks now, little flutters at first, but they've been getting stronger as time goes by, and I love it when my child bumps against my hand.

I hear the strong heartbeat and then the ultrasound tech looks over at us with a little smile.

"Do you want to know the sex?" she asks.

I look at Aurora and Aurora looks back at me. "Do we?" she asks, and I nod.

The tech points to the ultrasound. "It's a boy."

"A boy," I breathe, thinking about all the firsts: first steps, first words. The first time I teach him to ride a bike or drive a car, playing catch, his first drink. There's so much future to look forward to, and all I want to do is to share it with Aurora. If only she believed how much I love her.

I cry a little in spite of myself, and Aurora leans up to kiss me.

"You're going to be such a good father," she says, and I smile.

"You're going to be the best mother, *principessa*."

We head home and it's finally almost time that we can make love again. We cuddle in the bed and I grow hard behind her, pressing my hips into her ass.

"We can't," Aurora complains. "Not until you're better."

"I'm better," I tell her. "I'm down to one of the pain pills a day, even, Aurora, when are you going to let me tell you—"

She cuts me off with a kiss, pushing me down onto the bed and straddling my hips, and I stop thinking.

She rolls her hips slowly against me, leaning down to kiss my neck, and I groan, aching for her.

"Don't tease me, *principessa*. It's been so long."

It's been *too* long. It takes too long to recover from open-heart surgery and I hate having to wait. I sleep next to her every night and I want her so badly.

Aurora hums. "But maybe it's kind of fun to tease you," she murmurs.

This is a new side to Aurora, the way she's taking charge, and I have to admit that I like it.

She pulls down my sweats, freeing me, and I'm so hard I could cut diamond.

Aurora wraps her small fingers around me and I nearly come off the bed, thrusting into her hand and panting.

"Do you want me?" she asks, and I hitch in a breath.

"God, yes. Want you so badly. Want to be buried inside you right now."

"I want you, too," she admits, her brown eyes dark with lust.

She's wearing a little sundress that pulls tight over her baby bump, and god, she looks so sexy.

I reach up and tug it off her, making her breasts bounce free. She's just gotten curvier since she's been pregnant, and I love it.

Aurora doesn't waste time, slowly lowering herself down on me and I moan so loudly they can probably hear me in upstate New York.

"Oh, fuck," I gasp, taking hold of her hips in my hand, bouncing her on my dick.

"Fuck," Aurora agrees, rolling her hips. "You feel so good, Nico."

"I bet you feel better," I manage. "So slick and hot, tight around me."

"God, Nico, wish you could flip me over," she murmurs, and then I grab her hips and do it, ignoring the ache in my chest.

The doctor cleared me for sex last week, and we just haven't had the time. It was my main question to him and he thought it was funny, but I didn't.

"Nico!" she yelps, but I just slide back into her, rolling my hips quickly, just chasing my own orgasm.

She begins to gasp under me as I kiss along her neck, slamming my pelvis into hers, grinding against her clit.

"I'm going to come, Nico, oh, god," she whimpers, and then she explodes around me, pulsing, making me shout.

I spill inside of her after a few more thrusts, feeling like I've emptied my soul into her.

I slowly pull out and she whines at the loss, so I kiss all along her collarbone.

"Sorry," I murmur. "Couldn't help myself."

She giggles. "That's okay. I loved it," she admits.

"Of course you did. Dirty girl."

I slide my fingers down her belly and then hook my fingers into her, keeping my seed inside her and she gasps.

"Don't," she warns. "I'm sensitive."

"Sensitive is good," I mumble. "Let me make you come again. Once isn't enough."

She rocks her hips against my fingers and I know I have the okay, pumping them in and out of her.

Aurora looks so sexy like this, all swollen with my baby, her breasts bouncing, her body arching.

"You take my fingers so well, *principessa*," I praise, and she groans.

"I'm so close already," she gasps.

I smirk and slowly pump my fingers, wanting to draw out her orgasm, and after she comes, I pull out my fingers and pop them into my mouth, tasting both of us on them.

"You call me dirty," she laughs, and I snort and plop down beside her.

"I love you," I tell her, like I tell her every day, and Aurora frowns.

"I keep telling you not to say that yet."

"Aurora," I groan. "I'm down to one painkiller a day, in the mornings. I'm not on any drugs. I'm not out of my mind. I love you, and I want you to know it."

She bites her lip as I put my arms around her and her nose brushes against mine.

"You really mean it?" she asks.

"Of course I mean it," I say softly. "You're having my baby and I want you both, forever."

"Forever?" she asks.

I lick my lips. "I wanted to keep this a surprise for later, but..."

I roll over and reach for the nightstand. I pull open the drawer and take out the ring, turning toward her to let her see it.

It's one carat, inlaid with three other diamonds, and she gasps, her eyes filling with tears.

"You're not serious," she says.

"I'm serious as a heart attack," I joke, and she smacks my arm.

"Don't joke about that."

"*Principessa*," I say softly, cupping her face with my hand as she admires the ring. "I want to marry you."

"I thought you said baby steps."

"Changed my mind and want big boy steps," I insist, and she chuckles, still looking at the ring. "Look at me, *principessa*."

She catches my eye, her own brown eyes wide and wet.

"I love you," I say again, fiercely. "I'd die for you and my son, and I want you to come down the aisle in a dress and prove to me that we'll all be together forever. Will you marry me?"

Aurora stares at me for the longest time and then she lets me put the ring on her finger.

"I'll marry you, Nico," she says, and I kiss her so hard it almost bruises both our lips.

After that, she believes me when I tell her that I love her. She knows it, just like I do, knows that we'll all three be together forever.

I've still got a new scars, a zipper down to my belly button, but we'll be scarred together and everything will be okay.

33

AURORA

The day of the wedding, everything goes wrong.

It's raining and Francesca is late and I don't know if I can go through with this.

She finally shows up and her hair looks mussed and I groan.

"I know you've got a man, you should just tell me," I say, and she laughs.

"Absolutely not. I just overslept. I've been single and with me, myself, and I," she insists. "I'm so sorry, Aurora."

I haven't seen Nico in three days and I miss him so much. We've been living together but I've been staying with my father for the last two days according to tradition.

"I feel like I'm too pregnant for this dress," I say.

"You look beautiful. Nico is going to lose it the second he sees you," she insists.

In fact, when I walk down the aisle with Papa, Nico has a tear running down his cheek.

"This dress is perfect," he murmurs to me, and it reminds me of that first night, the first night he really noticed me in that dress, and I can't help but smile, happy tears pricking at the backs of my eyes.

I'm just about eight months pregnant and I feel like I'm about to burst out of the seams of the dress I'm in, but if Nico thinks I look perfect, then I feel perfect.

I barely listen as the priest says we can do our own vows, and I fumble when I take the notes I wrote from Francesca.

"Nico," I start, and then I just hand the notes back to her. "I wrote so many beautiful words about how much I love you and how grateful I am that you're with me and our baby, but it seems like too little. I've been in love with you for as long as I can remember, and I'm just so happy that you chose me."

"I'll keep choosing you," he says. "Every day, for the rest of our lives." He takes in a shaky breath. "Aurora. *Principessa.* I can't believe that I've known you for so long and for some crazy reason, I never realized how amazing you are. You've got such a big heart and soul, and all I can say is that I'm so happy that *you* chose *me*. You could have anyone you want, with that big heart and that perfect face of yours, and you chose me all those years ago. I'm sorry it took me so long to notice."

I'm crying in earnest now, and he takes my hand, slides the ring on it.

"Will you say I do, *principessa*, and believe me when I say that I love you? When I say that you're beautiful? Will you say that you'll be with me forever?"

"I'm yours, Nico," I tell him. "I've always been yours."

I shakily slide the ring on his finger and he leans down to kiss me before the priest says that he can kiss the bride.

He grins sheepishly when he looks back up, and Francesca laughs.

I'm the one that kisses him when the priest finally says it, and everyone in audience cheers.

Dante and Mia hold the reception at their place, and it's beautiful, flowers everywhere.

Francesca comes up to me with a glass of champagne and hugs me tightly.

"You looked amazing up there," she says, and I smile at her, patting her back. "We've been through so much but you handled it with such grace."

"So, now can I be mad at you for getting me into that situation?" I ask with a laugh to let her know I'm not serious.

"Absolutely not," she says. "That's how my stupid brother fell in love with you."

I blink at her, knowing that she's right. That *is* how Nico and I fell in love.

"I guess you're right. Thank you for almost getting me killed," I joke, and Francesca cackles and hugs me again.

We're cutting the cake when my stomach begins to cramp.

"I think I ate too many crab cakes," I mutter.

"Are you okay, *principessa*?" Nico asks with a concerned look, and I nod slowly, straightening up.

When I do, it's like pain tears across my stomach and I let out a little scream.

Mia hands off their baby girl to Dante and rushes toward me.

"Is it like there's a vice around your stomach?" she asks, and I nod. Her face pales and she looks over at Dante.

"We're going to the hospital," she says, and Nico blanches.

"What? Why? It's not time. It's too early," he insists.

"Babies don't care if it's too early," Mia insists. "We have to go. *Now.*"

The pain gets worse and worse and then at the hospital, my wedding dress soaks with blood at the crotch, and the doctors wheel me to the delivery room.

They can't find the baby's heartbeat and my heart is in my chest. Nico's right next to me, clutching my hand.

"The baby's in distress," the doctor says quickly. "We have to do a c-section. Right now."

"What? Not now," I plead. "He's not big enough. He's not ready."

"We don't have a choice," the doctor insists, and Nico looks down at me.

"It's going to be okay, *principessa*," he says, but his face is pale and drawn.

"I don't know if I can do this," I whisper shakily. "What if something's wrong? Really wrong?"

"He's going to be fine," he insists, as if convincing himself. "And you're going to be fine and we're going to be happy."

I swallow and then the doctor's give me some kind of drug to calm me down and everything seems floaty. I only feel pressure when they take out the baby but Nico gasps, tears streaming down his face.

"What does he look like?" I ask, and Nico's voice shakes when he answers.

"Perfect," he says. "He looks perfect, *principessa*. You did such a good job." He leans down to kiss me.

I don't hear our baby crying and I'm panicking, my throat tight, my chest aching as if I can't get enough oxygen.

"Take deep breaths, Ms. Costa," the doctor says.

"Andretti," Nico corrects. "Now it's Andretti."

"Mrs. Andretti," the doctor repeats. "Your oxygen levels are low and we need to take the baby to the NICU."

"Is he okay?" I ask as the doctors put the oxygen mask over my face.

"He's okay," Nico says, but I'm not sure that he knows.

I fade out of consciousness and the next thing I know, Nico is clutching my hand at my bedside.

"Our son," I ask immediately when I come through. "I need my son to be okay."

"He's perfect," Nico says again, sniffling, and I realize that he's been crying. "He's doing fine in the NICU, breathing well. Just not much of a crier, I guess."

"And me?" I ask, looking down at myself. My stomach aches and I feel sore all over.

"You lost a lot of blood," he says. "They didn't know if you would make it, and *principessa*..." He trails off and chokes out a sob. "I thought I lost you."

"You didn't," I tell him, squeezing his hand. "I'm here."

I recover in the hospital and get to meet my son.

"What are we going to call him?" I ask, looking down at his little face, at the way he has his father's nose and chin.

"I thought Aldo was a strong name," he says, and I smile down at our son.

"Aldo," I say, liking the sound of it. "I think that's perfect, Nico."

"I think you're perfect," Nico says, and I can't believe this is my life. I can't believe that I have my son and that Nico Andretti is my husband.

It's all I've ever wanted.

After we're home, our baby finds his voice and screams the night away, but just when I think I'm getting to my breaking point, Nico's there.

"I'll take him for a while," he says, pulling our son out of my arms.

I run a hand through my mussed hair, exhausted. "He was crying all night," I say.

"Why didn't you wake me?" he asks, frowning.

"You looked so peaceful," I tell him. "I didn't want to disturb you."

Nico snorts. "Disturb me next time, *principessa*. I'm his father. I can do a lot of the work."

I look at him, disbelieving. I can't believe he's so involved when at first, I didn't even know if he'd stick around even if he said he would.

"I'm exhausted," I admit. "And there's baby vomit in my hair and I'm pretty sure his diaper is full of the most heinous thing you've ever smelled."

Nico barks out a surprised laugh. "I'm interested in where this is going."

"But I'm so *happy*, Nico," I said, tears running down my face. "I've never been so happy in all my life. I didn't know I could find happiness like this."

"Me, either," Nico says, kissing the tip of my nose. "This is everything, and I never knew I wanted any of it."

Baby Aldo has finally stopped crying and now he's just looking around as if he hasn't kept me up all night and driven me crazy.

"And we can do this," I say, determined.

Nico grins at me. "We can do this, even if I have to bounce this kid around twenty-four hours a day."

It's not easy because Aldo has colic and I have to recover from surgery.

Sometimes I'm bitchy because Aldo's been up for hours and I haven't had anything to eat or any sleep.

On those days, Nico takes over, taking the baby for several hours and sending me to the spa with Francesca, who is the world's best aunt.

I look in the mirror in the mornings and I can't believe this is my life. I can't believe I'm so happy.

Nico tells me, every day, that he feels the same way. He never minds reassuring me, never minds telling me over and over that he loves me. Sometimes, when we're making love, he'll trail his fingers over the scar on my cheekbone or my c-section scar, and he'll tell me that everything we've been through has been so worth it.

"*So* worth it, *principessa*," he says softly. "Everything has been so worth it, and I love you so fucking much."

I grin, looking back at him and then looking over at our son in the bassinet next to our bed. He's only quiet when Nico and I are together, when we're in the same room, like he knows that we're all three meant to be together.

"Everything was worth it, but did it have to be *so* hard?" I ask, and Nico laughs, loud and open.

Most days, I can't believe it when I wake up next to Nico, our baby crying over the baby monitor or from the bassinet. I can't believe it, but Nico convinces me, every single day.

I'm Mrs. Andretti, and we have a beautiful baby boy, and Nico Andretti loves me with every cell of his body.

What else could I ever need?